Dante

The Descent into Hell

TRANSLATED BY DOROTHY L. SAYERS

PENGUIN EPICS

PENGUIN BOOKS

Published by the Penguin Group
Penguin Books Ltd, 80 Strand, London WC2R ORL, England
Penguin Group (USA) Inc., 375 Hudson Street, New York, New York 10014, USA
Penguin Group (Canada), 90 Eglinton Avenue East, Suite 700, Toronto, Ontario, Canada M4P 2Y3
(a division of Pearson Penguin Canada Inc.)
Penguin Ireland, 25 St Stephen's Green, Dublin 2, Ireland (a division of Penguin Books Ltd)
Penguin Group (Australia), 250 Camberwell Road, Camberwell, Victoria 3124, Australia
(a division of Pearson Australia Group Pty Ltd)
Penguin Books India Pvt Ltd, 11 Community Centre, Panchsheel Park, New Delhi – 110 017, India
Penguin Group (NZ), cnr Airborne and Rosedale Roads, Albany,
Auckland 1310, New Zealand (a division of Pearson New Zealand Ltd)
Penguin Books (South Africa) (Pty) Ltd, 24 Sturdee Avenue,
Rosebank, Johannesburg 2196, South Africa

Penguin Books Ltd, Registered Offices: 80 Strand, London WC2R ORL, England

www.penguin.com

This translation of Dante's *Inferno* first published 1949
This extract published in Penguin Books 2006

1

Translation copyright 1949 by Dorothy L. Sayers
All rights reserved

The moral right of the translator has been asserted

Typeset by Rowland Phototypesetting Ltd, Bury St Edmunds, Suffolk
Printed in England by Clays Ltd, St Ives plc

ISBN-13: 978-0-141-02642-8
ISBN-10: 0-141-02642-1

Contents

Note

The extracts published here as *The Descent into Hell* are taken from the *Inferno*, the first of three books that make up *The Divine Comedy* (the other books being *Purgatory* and *Paradise*). *The Divine Comedy*, Dante Alighieri's poetic masterpiece, was written in the early fourteenth century.

Canto I

The Story. *Dante finds that he has strayed from the right road and is lost in a Dark Wood. He tries to escape by climbing a beautiful Mountain, but is turned aside, first by a gambolling Leopard, then by a fierce Lion, and finally by a ravenous She-Wolf. As he is fleeing back into the wood, he is stopped by the shade of Virgil, who tells him that he cannot hope to pass the Wolf and ascend the Mountain by that road. One day a Greyhound will come and drive the Wolf back to Hell; but the only course at present left open to Dante is to trust himself to Virgil, who will guide him by a longer way, leading through Hell and Purgatory. From there, a worthier spirit than Virgil (Beatrice) will lead him on to see the blessed souls in Paradise. Dante accepts Virgil as his 'master, leader, and lord', and they set out together.*

Midway this way of life we're bound upon,
   I woke to find myself in a dark wood,
   Where the right road was wholly lost and gone.

Ay me! how hard to speak of it – that rude
   And rough and stubborn forest! the mere breath
   Of memory stirs the old fear in the blood;

It is so bitter, it goes nigh to death;
    Yet there I gained such good, that, to convey
    The tale, I'll write what else I found therewith.

How I got into it I cannot say,
    Because I was so heavy and full of sleep
    When first I stumbled from the narrow way;

But when at last I stood beneath a steep
    Hill's side, which closed that valley's wandering maze
    Whose dread had pierced me to the heart-root deep,

Then I looked up, and saw the morning rays
    Mantle its shoulder from that planet bright
    Which guides men's feet aright on all their ways;

And this a little quieted the affright
    That lurking in my bosom's lake had lain
    Through the long horror of that piteous night.

And as a swimmer, panting, from the main
    Heaves safe to shore, then turns to face the drive
    Of perilous seas, and looks, and looks again,

So, while my soul yet fled, did I contrive
    To turn and gaze on that dread pass once more
    Whence no man yet came ever out alive.

Weary of limb I rested a brief hour,
    Then rose and onward through the desert hied,
    So that the fixed foot always was the lower;

And see! not far from where the mountain-side
　　First rose, a Leopard, nimble and light and fleet,
　　Clothed in a fine furred pelt all dapple-dyed,

Came gambolling out, and skipped before my feet,
　　Hindering me so, that from the forthright line
　　Time and again I turned to beat retreat.

The morn was young, and in his native sign
　　The Sun climbed with the stars whose glitterings
　　Attended on him when the Love Divine

First moved those happy, prime-created things:
　　So the sweet season and the new-born day
　　Filled me with hope and cheerful augurings

Of the bright beast so speckled and so gay;
　　Yet not so much but that I fell to quaking
　　At a fresh sight – a Lion in the way.

I saw him coming, swift and savage, making
　　For me, head high, with ravenous hunger raving
　　So that for dread the very air seemed shaking.

And next, a Wolf, gaunt with the famished craving
　　Lodged ever in her horrible lean flank,
　　The ancient cause of many men's enslaving; –

She was the worst – at that dread sight a blank
　　Despair and whelming terror pinned me fast,
　　Until all hope to scale the mountain sank.

Like one who loves the gains he has amassed,
    And meets the hour when he must lose his loot,
    Distracted in his mind and all aghast,

Even so was I, faced with that restless brute
    Which little by little edged and thrust me back,
    Back, to that place wherein the sun is mute.

Then, as I stumbled headlong down the track,
    Sudden a form was there, which dumbly crossed
    My path, as though grown voiceless from long lack

Of speech; and seeing it in that desert lost,
    'Have pity on me!' I hailed it as I ran,
    'Whate'er thou art – or very man, or ghost!'

It spoke: 'No man, although I once was man;
    My parents' native land was Lombardy
    And both by citizenship were Mantuan.

Sub Julio born, though late in time, was I,
    And lived at Rome in good Augustus' days,
    When the false gods were worshipped ignorantly.

Poet was I, and tuned my verse to praise
    Anchises' righteous son, who sailed from Troy
    When Ilium's pride fell ruined down ablaze.

But thou – oh, why run back where fears destroy
    Peace? Why not climb the blissful mountain yonder,
    The cause and first beginning of all joy?'

'Canst thou be Virgil? thou that fount of splendour
   Whence poured so wide a stream of lordly speech?'
   Said I, and bowed my awe-struck head in wonder;

'O honour and light of poets all and each,
   Now let my great love stead me – the bent brow
   And long hours pondering all thy book can teach!

Thou art my master, and my author thou,
   From thee alone I learned the singing strain,
   The noble style, that does me honour now.

See there the beast that turned me back again –
   Save me from her, great sage – I fear her so,
   She shakes my blood through every pulse and vein.'

'Nay, by another path thou needs must go
   If thou wilt ever leave this waste,' he said,
   Looking upon me as I wept, 'for lo!

The savage brute that makes thee cry for dread
   Lets no man pass this road of hers, but still
   Trammels him, till at last she lays him dead.

Vicious her nature is, and framed for ill;
   When crammed she craves more fiercely than before;
   Her raging greed can never gorge its fill.

With many a beast she mates, and shall with more,
   Until the Greyhound come, the Master-hound,
   And he shall slay her with a stroke right sore.

He'll not eat gold nor yet devour the ground;
  Wisdom and love and power his food shall be,
  His birthplace between Feltro and Feltro found;

Saviour he'll be to that low Italy
  For which Euryalus and Nisus died,
  Turnus and chaste Camilla, bloodily.

He'll hunt the Wolf through cities far and wide,
  Till in the end he hunt her back to Hell,
  Whence Envy first of all her leash untied.

But, as for thee, I think and deem it well
  Thou take me for thy guide, and pass with me
  Through an eternal place and terrible

Where thou shalt hear despairing cries, and see
  Long-parted souls that in their torments dire
  Howl for the second death perpetually.

Next, thou shalt gaze on those who in the fire
  Are happy, for they look to mount on high,
  In God's good time, up to the blissful quire;

To which glad place, a worthier spirit than I
  Must lead thy steps, if thou desire to come,
  With whom I'll leave thee then, and say good-bye;

For the Emperor of that high Imperium
  Wills not that I, once rebel to His crown,
  Into that city of His should lead men home.

Everywhere is His realm, but there His throne,
   There is His city and exalted seat:
   Thrice-blest whom there He chooses for His own!'

Then I to him: 'Poet, I thee entreat,
   By that great God whom thou didst never know,
   Lead on, that I may free my wandering feet

From these snares and from worse; and I will go
   Along with thee, St Peter's Gate to find,
   And those whom thou portray'st as suffering so.'

So he moved on; and I moved on behind.

Canto II

The Story. Dante's attempts to climb the Mountain have taken the whole day and it is now Good Friday evening. Dante has not gone far before he loses heart and 'begins to make excuse'. To his specious arguments Virgil replies flatly: 'This is mere cowardice;' and then tells how Beatrice, prompted by St Lucy at the instance of the Virgin Mary herself, descended into Limbo to entreat him to go to Dante's rescue. Thus encouraged, Dante pulls himself together, and they start off again.

Day was departing and the dusk drew on,
    Loosing from labour every living thing
    Save me, in all the world; I – I alone –

Must gird me to the wars – rough travelling,
    And pity's sharp assault upon the heart –
    Which memory shall record, unfaltering;

Now, Muses, now, high Genius, do your part!
    And Memory, faithful scrivener to the eyes,
    Here show thy virtue, noble as thou art!

I soon began: 'Poet – dear guide – 'twere wise
    Surely, to test my powers and weigh their worth
    Ere trusting me to this great enterprise.

Thou sayest, the author of young Silvius' birth,
    Did to the world immortal, mortal go,
    Clothed in the body of flesh he wore on earth –

Granted; if Hell's great Foeman deigned to show
    To *him* such favour, seeing the vast effect,
    And what and who his destined issue – no,

That need surprise no thoughtful intellect,
    Since to Rome's fostering city and empery
    High Heaven had sealed him as the father-elect;

Both these were there established, verily,
    To found that place, holy and dedicate,
    Wherein great Peter's heir should hold his See;

So that the deed thy verses celebrate
    Taught him the road to victory, and bestowed
    The Papal Mantle in its high estate.

Thither the Chosen Vessel, in like mode,
    Went afterward, and much confirmed thereby
    The faith that sets us on salvation's road.

But how should *I* go there? Who says so? Why?
    I'm not Aeneas, and I am not Paul!
    Who thinks me fit? Not others. And not I.

Say I submit, and go – suppose I fall
    Into some folly? Though I speak but ill,
    Thy better wisdom will construe it all.'

As one who wills, and then unwills his will,
    Changing his mind with every changing whim,
    Till all his best intentions come to nil,

So I stood havering in that moorland dim,
    While through fond rifts of fancy oozed away
    The first quick zest that filled me to the brim.

'If I have grasped what thou dost seem to say,'
    The shade of greatness answered, 'these doubts breed
    From sheer black cowardice, which day by day

Lays ambushes for men, checking the speed
    Of honourable purpose in mid-flight,
    As shapes half-seen startle a shying steed.

Well then, to rid thee of this foolish fright,
    Hear why I came, and learn whose eloquence
    Urged me to take compassion on thy plight.

While I was with the spirits who dwell suspense,
    A Lady summoned me – so blest, so rare,
    I begged her to command my diligence.

Her eyes outshone the firmament by far
    As she began, in her own gracious tongue,
    Gentle and low, as tongues of angels are:

"O courteous Mantuan soul, whose skill in song
    Keeps green on earth a fame that shall not end
    While motion rolls the turning spheres along!

A friend of mine, who is not Fortune's friend,
   Is hard beset upon the shadowy coast;
   Terrors and snares his fearful steps attend,

Driving him back; yea, and I fear almost
   I have risen too late to help – for I was told
   Such news of him in Heaven – he's too far lost.

But thou – go thou! Lift up thy voice of gold;
   Try every needful means to find and reach
   And free him, that my heart may rest consoled.

Beatrice am I, who thy good speed beseech;
   Love that first moved me from the blissful place
   Whither I'd fain return, now moves my speech.

Lo! when I stand before my Lord's bright face
   I'll praise thee many a time to Him." Thereon
   She fell on silence; I replied apace:

"Excellent lady, for whose sake alone
   The breed of men exceeds all things that dwell
   Closed in the Heaven whose circles narrowest run

To do thy bidding pleases me so well
   That were't already done, I should seem slow;
   I know thy wish, and more needs not to tell.

Yet say – how can thy blest feet bear to know
   This dark road downward to the dreadful centre,
   From that wide room which thou dost yearn for so?"

"Few words will serve (if thou desire to enter
    Thus far into our mystery)," she said,
    "To tell thee why I have no fear to venture.

Of hurtful things we ought to be afraid,
    But of no others, truly, inasmuch
    As these have nothing to give cause for dread;

My nature, by God's mercy, is made such
    As your calamities can nowise shake,
    Nor these dark fires have any power to touch.

Heaven hath a noble Lady, who doth take
    Ruth of this man thou goest to disensnare
    Such that high doom is cancelled for her sake.

She summoned Lucy to her side, and there
    Exhorted her: 'Thy faithful votary
    Needs thee, and I commend him to thy care.'

Lucy, the foe to every cruelty,
    Ran quickly and came and found me in my place
    Beside ancestral Rachel, crying to me:

'How now, how now, Beatrice, God's true praise!
    No help for him who once thy liegeman was,
    Quitting the common herd to win thy grace?

Dost thou not hear his piteous cries, alas?
    Dost thou not see death grapple him, on the river
    Whose furious rage no ocean can surpass?'

When I heard that, no living wight was ever
  So swift to seek his good or flee his fear
  As I from that high resting-place to sever

And speed me down, trusting my purpose dear
  To thee, and to thy golden rhetoric
  Which honours thee, and honours all who hear."

She spoke; and as she turned from me the quick
  Tears starred the lustre of her eyes, which still
  Spurred on my going with a keener prick.

Therefore I sought thee out, as was her will,
  And brought thee safe off from that beast of prey
  Which barred thee from the short road up the hill.

What ails thee then? Why, why this dull delay?
  Why bring so white a liver to the deed?
  Why canst thou find no manhood to display

When three such blessed ladies deign to plead
  Thy cause at that supreme assize of right,
  And when my words promise thee such good speed?'

As little flowers, which all the frosty night
  Hung pinched and drooping, lift their stalks and fan
  Their blossoms out, touched by the warm white light,

So did my fainting powers; and therewith ran
  Such good, strong courage round about my heart
  That I spoke boldly out like a free man:

'O blessed she that stooped to take my part!
  O courteous thou, to obey her true-discerning
  Speech, and thus promptly to my rescue start!

Fired by thy words, my spirit now is burning
  So to go on, and see this venture through
  I find my former stout resolve returning.

Forward! henceforth there's but one will for two,
  Thou master, and thou leader, and thou lord.'
  I spoke; he moved; so, setting out anew,

I entered on that savage path and froward.

Canto III

The Story. *Arriving at the gate of Hell, the Poets read the inscription upon its lintel. They enter and find themselves in the Vestibule of Hell, where the Futile run perpetually after a whirling standard. Passing quickly on, they reach the river Acheron. Here the souls of all the damned come at death to be ferried across by Charon, who refuses to take the living body of Dante till Virgil silences him with a word of power. While they are watching the departure of a boatload of souls the river banks are shaken by an earthquake so violent that Dante swoons away.*

THROUGH ME THE ROAD TO THE CITY OF DESOLATION,
    THROUGH ME THE ROAD TO SORROWS DIUTURNAL,
    THROUGH ME THE ROAD AMONG THE LOST CREATION.

JUSTICE MOVED MY GREAT MAKER; GOD ETERNAL
    WROUGHT ME: THE POWER, AND THE UNSEARCHABLY
    HIGH WISDOM, AND THE PRIMAL LOVE SUPERNAL.

NOTHING ERE I WAS MADE WAS MADE TO BE
    SAVE THINGS ETERNE, AND I ETERNE ABIDE;
    LAY DOWN ALL HOPE, YOU THAT GO IN BY ME.

These words, of sombre colour, I descried
    Writ on the lintel of a gateway; 'Sir,
    This sentence is right hard for me,' I cried.

And like a man of quick discernment: 'Here
    Lay down all thy distrust,' said he, 'reject
    Dead from within thee every coward fear;

We've reached the place I told thee to expect,
    Where thou shouldst see the miserable race,
    Those who have lost the good of intellect.'

He laid his hand on mine, and with a face
    So joyous that it comforted my quailing,
    Into the hidden things he led my ways.

Here sighing, and here crying, and loud railing
    Smote on the starless air, with lamentation,
    So that at first I wept to hear such wailing.

Tongues mixed and mingled, horrible execration,
    Shrill shrieks, hoarse groans, fierce yells and hideous
      blether
    And clapping of hands thereto, without cessation

Made tumult through the timeless night, that hither
    And thither drives in dizzying circles sped,
    As whirlwind whips the spinning sands together.

Whereat, with horror flapping round my head:
   'Master, what's this I hear? Who can they be,
   These people so distraught with grief?' I said.

And he replied: 'The dismal company
   Of wretched spirits thus find their guerdon due
   Whose lives knew neither praise nor infamy;

They're mingled with that caitiff angle-crew
   Who against God rebelled not, nor to Him
   Were faithful, but to self alone were true;

Heaven cast them forth – their presence there would dim
   The light; deep Hell rejects so base a herd,
   Lest sin should boast itself because of them.

Then I: 'But, Master, by what torment spurred
   Are they driven on to vent such bitter breath?'
   He answered: 'I will tell thee in a word:

This dreary huddle has no hope of death,
   Yet its blind life trails on so low and crass
   That every other fate it envieth.

No reputation in the world it has,
   Mercy and doom hold it alike in scorn –
   Let us not speak of these; but look, and pass.'

So I beheld, and lo! an ensign borne
   Whirling, that span and ran, as in disdain
   Of any rest; and there the folk forlorn

Rushed after it, in such an endless train,
  It never would have entered in my head
  There were so many men whom death had slain.

And when I'd noted here and there a shade
  Whose face I knew, I saw and recognised
  The coward spirit of the man who made

The great refusal; and that proof sufficed;
  Here was that rabble, here without a doubt,
  Whom God and whom His enemies despised.

This scum, who'd never lived, now fled about
  Naked and goaded, for a swarm of fierce
  Hornets and wasps stung all the wretched rout

Until their cheeks ran blood, whose slubbered smears,
  Mingled with brine, around their footsteps fell,
  Where loathly worms licked up their blood and tears.

Then I peered on ahead, and soon quite well
  Made out the hither bank of a wide stream,
  Where stood much people. 'Sir,' said I, 'pray tell

Who these are, what their custom, why they seem
  So eager to pass over and be gone –
  If I may trust my sight in this pale gleam.'

And he to me: 'The whole shall be made known;
  Only have patience till we stay our feet
  On yonder sorrowful shore of Acheron.'

Abashed, I dropped my eyes; and, lest unmeet
   Chatter should vex him, held my tongue, and so
   Paced on with him, in silence and discreet,

To the riverside. When from the far bank lo!
   A boat shot forth, whose white-haired boatman old
   Bawled as he came: 'Woe to the wicked! Woe!

Never you hope to look on Heaven – behold!
   I come to ferry you hence across the tide
   To endless night, fierce fires and shramming cold.

And thou, the living man there! stand aside
   From these who are dead!' I budged not, but abode;
   So, when he saw me hold my ground, he cried:

'Away with thee! for by another road
   And other ferries thou shalt make the shore,
   Not here; a lighter skiff must bear thy load.'

Then said my guide: 'Charon, why wilt thou roar
   And chafe in vain? Thus it is willed where power
   And will are one; enough; ask thou no more.'

This shut the shaggy mouth up of that sour
   Infernal ferryman of the livid wash,
   Only his flame-ringed eyeballs rolled a-glower.

But those outwearied, naked souls – how gash
   And pale they grew, chattering their teeth for dread,
   When first they felt his harsh tongue's cruel lash.

God they blaspheme, blaspheme their parents' bed,
  The human race, the place, the time, the blood,
  The seed that got them, and the womb that bred;

Then, huddling hugger-mugger, down they scud,
  Dismally wailing, to the accursed strand
  Which waits for every man that fears not God.

Charon, his eyes red like a burning brand,
  Thumps with his oar the lingerers that delay,
  And rounds them up, and beckons with his hand.

And as, by one and one, leaves drift away
  In autumn, till the bough from which they fall
  Sees the earth strewn with all its brave array,

So, from the bank there, one by one, drop all
  Adam's ill seed, when signalled off the mark,
  As drops the falcon to the falconer's call.

Away they're borne across the waters dark,
  And ere they land that side the stream, anon
  Fresh troops this side come flocking to embark;

Then said my courteous master: 'See, my son,
  All those that die beneath God's righteous ire
  From every country come here every one.

They press to pass the river, for the fire
  Of heavenly justice stings and spurs them so
  That all their fear is changed into desire;

And by this passage, good souls never go;
    Therefore, if Charon chide thee, do thou look
    What this may mean – 'tis not so hard to know.'

When he thus said, the dusky champaign shook
    So terribly that, thinking on the event,
    I feel the sweat pour off me like a brook.

The sodden ground belched wind, and through the rent
    Shot the red levin, with a flash and sweep
    That robbed me of my wits, incontinent;

And down I fell, as one that swoons on sleep.

Canto IV

The Story. *Recovering from his swoon, Dante finds himself across Acheron and on the edge of the actual Pit of Hell. He follows Virgil into the First Circle – the Limbo where the Unbaptized and the Virtuous Pagans dwell 'suspended', knowing no torment save exclusion from the positive bliss of God's presence. Virgil tells him of Christ's Harrowing of Hell, and then shows him the habitation of the great men of antiquity – poets, heroes, and philosophers.*

A heavy peal of thunder came to waken me
  Out of the stunning slumber that had bound me,
  Startling me up as though rude hands had shaken me.

I rose, and cast my rested eyes around me,
  Gazing intent to satisfy my wonder
  Concerning the strange place wherein I found me.

Hear truth: I stood on the steep brink whereunder
  Runs down the dolorous chasm of the Pit,
  Ringing with infinite groans like gathered thunder.

Deep, dense, and by no faintest glimmer lit
  It lay, and though I strained my sight to find
  Bottom, not one thing could I see in it.

'Down must we go, to that dark world and blind,'
    The poet said, turning on me a bleak
    Blanched face; 'I will go first – come thou behind.'

Then I, who had marked the colour of his cheek:
    'How can I go, when even thou art white
    For fear, who art wont to cheer me when I'm weak?'

But he: 'Not so; the anguish infinite
    They suffer yonder paints my countenance
    With pity, which thou takest for affright;

Come, we have far to go; let us advance.'
    So, entering, he made me enter, where
    The Pit's first circle makes circumference.

We heard no loud complaint, no crying there,
    No sound of grief except the sound of sighing
    Quivering for ever through the eternal air;

Grief, not for torment, but for loss undying,
    By women, men, and children sighed for so,
    Sorrowers thick-throned, their sorrows multiplying.

Then my good guide: 'Thou dost not ask me who
    These spirits are,' said he, 'whom thou perceivest?
    Ere going further, I would have thee know

They sinned not; yet their merit lacked its chiefest
    Fulfilment, lacking baptism, which is
    The gateway to the faith which thou believest;

Or, living before Christendom, their knees
   Paid not aright those tributes that belong
   To God; and I myself am one of these.

For such defects alone – no other wrong –
   We are lost; yet only by this grief offended:
   That, without hope, we ever live, and long.'

Grief smote my heart to think, as he thus ended,
   What souls I knew, of great and soveran
   Virtue, who in that Limbo dwelt suspended.

'Tell me, sir – tell me, Master,' I began
   (In hope some fresh assurance to be gleaning
   Of our sin-conquering Faith), 'did any man

By his self-merit, or on another leaning,
   Ever fare forth from hence and come to be
   Among the blest?' He took my hidden meaning.

'When I was newly in this state,' said he,
   'I saw One come in majesty and awe,
   And on His head were crowns of victory.

Our great first father's spirit He did withdraw,
   And righteous Abel, Noah who built the ark,
   Moses who gave and who obeyed the Law,

King David, Abraham the Patriarch,
   Israel with his father and generation,
   Rachel, for whom he did such deeds of mark,

With many another of His chosen nation;
   These did He bless; and know, that ere that day
   No human soul had ever seen salvation.'

While he thus spake, we still made no delay,
   But passed the wood – I mean, the wood (as 'twere)
   Of souls ranged thick as trees. Being now some way –

Not far – from where I'd slept, I saw appear
   A light, which overcame the shadowy face
   Of gloom, and made a glowing hemisphere.

'Twas yet some distance on, yet I could trace
   So much as brought conviction to my heart
   That persons of great honour held that place.

'O thou that honour'st every science and art,
   Say, who are these whose honour gives them claim
   To different customs and a sphere apart?'

And he to me: 'Their honourable name,
   Still in thy world resounding as it does,
   Wins here from Heaven the favour due to fame.'

Meanwhile I heard a voice that cried out thus:
   'Honour the most high poet! his great shade,
   Which was departed, is returned to us.'

It paused there, and was still; and lo! there made
   Toward us, four mighty shadows of the dead,
   Who in their mien nor grief nor joy displayed.

'Mark well the first of these,' my master said,
  'Who in his right hand bears a naked sword
  And goes before the three as chief and head;

Homer is he, the poets' sovran lord;
  Next, Horace comes, the keen satirical;
  Ovid the third; and Lucan afterward.

Because I share with these that honourable
  Grand title the sole voice was heard to cry
  They do me honour, and therein do well.'

Thus in their school assembled I, even I,
  Looked on the lords of loftiest song, whose style
  O'er all the rest goes soaring eagle-high.

When they had talked together a short while
  They all with signs of welcome turned my way,
  Which moved my master to a kindly smile;

And greater honour yet they did me – yea,
  Into their fellowship they deigned invite
  And make me sixth among such minds as they.

So we moved slowly onward toward the light
  In talk 'twere as unfitting to repeat
  Here, as to speak there was both fit and right.

And presently we reached a noble seat –
  A castle, girt with seven high walls around,
  And moated with a goodly rivulet

O'er which we went as though upon dry ground;
    With those wise men I passed the sevenfold gate
    Into a fresh green meadow, where we found

Persons with grave and tranquil eyes, and great
    Authority in their carriage and attitude,
    Who spoke but seldom and in voice sedate.

So here we walked aside a little, and stood
    Upon an open eminence, lit serene
    And clear, whence one and all might well be viewed.

Plain in my sight on the enamelled green
    All those grand spirits were shown me one by one –
    It thrills my heart to think what I have seen!

I saw Electra, saw with her anon
    Hector, Aeneas, many a Trojan peer,
    And hawk-eyed Caesar in his habergeon;

I saw Camilla and bold Penthesilea,
    On the other hand; Latinus on his throne
    Beside Lavinia his daughter dear;

Brutus, by whom proud Tarquin was o'erthrown,
    Marcia, Cornelia, Julia, Lucrece – and
    I saw great Saladin, aloof, alone.

Higher I raised my brows and further scanned,
    And saw the Master of the men who know
    Seated amid the philosophic band;

All do him honour and deep reverence show;
   Socrates, Plato, in the nearest room
   To him; Diogenes, Thales and Zeno,

Democritus, who held that all things come
   By chance; Empedocles, Anaxagoras wise,
   And Heraclitus, him that wept for doom;

Dioscorides, who named the qualities,
   Tully and Orpheus, Linus, and thereby
   Good Seneca, well-skilled to moralise;

Euclid the geometrician, Ptolemy,
   Galen, Hippocrates, and Avicen,
   Averrhoës who made the commentary –

Nay, but I tell not all that I saw then;
   The long theme drives me hard, and everywhere
   The wondrous truth outstrips my staggering pen.

The group of six dwindles to two; we fare
   Forth a new way, I and my guide withal,
   Out from that quiet to the quivering air,

And reach a place where nothing shines at all.

Canto V

The Story. *Dante and Virgil descend from the First Circle to the Second (the first of the Circles of Incontinence). On the threshold sits Minos, the judge of Hell, assigning the souls to their appropriate places of torment. His opposition is overcome by Virgil's word of power, and the Poets enter the Circle, where the souls of the Lustful are tossed for ever upon a howling wind. After Virgil has pointed out a number of famous lovers, Dante speaks to the shade of Francesca da Rimini, who tells him her story.*

From the first circle thus I came descending
　　To the second, which, in narrower compass turning,
　　Holds greater woe, with outcry loud and rending.

There in the threshold, horrible and girning,
　　Grim Minos sits, holding his ghastly session,
　　And, as he girds him, sentencing and spurning;

For when the ill soul faces him, confession
　　Pours out of it till nothing's left to tell;
　　Whereon that connoisseur of all transgression

Assigns it to its proper place in Hell,
　　As many grades as he would have it fall,
　　So oft he belts him round with his own tail.

Before him stands a throng continual;
    Each comes in turn to abye the fell arraign;
    They speak – they hear – they're whirled down one
      and all.

'Ho! thou that comest to the house of pain,'
    Cried Minos when he saw me, the appliance
    Of his dread powers suspending, 'think again

How thou dost go, in whom is thy reliance;
    Be not deceived by the wide open door!'
    Then said my guide: 'Wherefore this loud
      defiance?

Hinder not thou his fated way; be sure
    Hindrance is vain; thus it is willed where will
    And power are one; enough; ask thou no more.'

And now the sounds of grief begin to fill
    My ear; I'm come where cries of anguish smite
    My shrinking sense, and lamentation shrill –

A place made dumb of every glimmer of light,
    Which bellows like tempestuous ocean birling
    In the batter of a two-way wind's buffet and fight.

The blast of Hell that never rests from whirling
    Harries the spirits along in the sweep of its swath,
    And vexes them, for ever beating and hurling.

When they are borne to the rim of the ruinous path
   With cry and wail and shriek they are caught by the
     gust,
   Railing and cursing the power of the Lord's wrath.

Into this torment carnal sinners are thrust,
   So I was told – the sinners who make their reason
   Bond thrall under the yoke of their lust.

Like as the starlings wheel in the wintry season
   In wide and clustering flocks wing-borne,
     wind borne
   Even so they go, the souls who did this treason,

Hither and thither, and up and down, outworn,
   Hopeless of any rest – rest, did I say?
   Of the least minishing of their pangs forlorn.

And as the cranes go chanting their harsh lay,
   Across the sky in long procession trailing,
   So I beheld some shadows borne my way,

Driven on the blast and uttering wail on wailing;
   Wherefore I said: 'O Master, art thou able
   To name these spirits thrashed by the black wind's
     flailing?'

'Among this band,' said he, 'whose name and fable
   Thou seek'st to know, the first who yonder flies
   Was empress of many tongues, mistress of Babel.

She was so broken to lascivious vice
   She licensed lust by law, in hopes to cover
   Her scandal of unnumbered harlotries.

This was Semiramis; 'tis written of her
   That she was wife to Ninus and heiress, too,
   Who reigned in the land the Soldan now rules over.

Lo! she that slew herself for love, untrue
   To Sychaeus' ashes. Lo! tost on the blast,
   Voluptuous Cleopatra, whom love slew.

Look, look on Helen, for whose sake rolled past
   Long evil years. See great Achilles yonder,
   Who warred with love, and that war was his last.

See Paris, Tristram see!' And many – oh, wonder
   Many – a thousand more, he showed by name
   And pointing hand, whose life love rent asunder.

And when I had heard my Doctor tell the fame
   Of all those knights and ladies of long ago,
   I was pierced through with pity, and my head
     swam.

'Poet,' said I, 'fain would I speak those two
   That seem to ride as light as any foam,
   And hand in hand on the dark wind drifting go.'

And he replied: 'Wait till they nearer roam,
  And thou shalt see; summon them to thy side
  By the power of the love that leads them, and they
    will come.'

So, as they eddied past on the whirling tide,
  I raised my voice: 'O souls that wearily rove,
  Come to us, speak to us – if it be not denied.'

And as desire wafts homeward dove with dove
  To their sweet nest, on raised and steady wing
  Down-dropping through the air, impelled by love,

So these from Dido's flock came fluttering
  And dropping toward us down the cruel wind,
  Such power was in my affectionate summoning.

'O living creature, gracious and so kind,
  Coming through this black air to visit us,
  Us, who in death the globe incarnadined,

Were the world's King our friend and might we thus
  Entreat, we would entreat Him for thy peace,
  That pitiest so our pangs dispiteous!

Hear all thou wilt, and speak as thou shalt please,
  And we will gladly speak with thee and hear,
  While the winds cease to howl, as they now cease.

There is a town upon the sea-coast, near
  Where Po with all his streams comes down to rest
  In ocean; I was born and nurtured there.

Love, that so soon takes hold in the gentle breast,
  Took this lad with the lovely body they tore
  From me; the way of it leaves me still distrest.

Love, that to no loved heart remits love's score,
  Took me with such great joy of him, that see!
  It holds me yet and never shall leave me more.

Love to a single death brought him and me;
  Cain's place lies waiting for our murderer now.'
  These words came wafted to us plaintively.

Hearing those wounded souls, I bent my brow
  Downward, and thus bemused I let time pass,
  Till the poet said at length: 'What thinkest thou?'

When I could answer, I began: 'Alas!
  Sweet thoughts how many, and desire how great,
  Brought down these twain unto the dolorous pass!'

And then I turned to them: 'Thy dreadful fate,
  Francesca, makes me weep, it so inspires
  Pity,' said I, 'and grief compassionate.

Tell me – in that time of sighing-sweet desires,
  How, and by what, did love his power disclose
  And grant you knowledge of your hidden fires?'

Then she to me: 'The bitterest woe of woes
    Is to remember in our wretchedness
    Old happy times; and this thy Doctor knows;

Yet, if so dear desire thy heart possess
    To know that root of love which wrought our fall,
    I'll be as those who weep and who confess.

One day we read for pastime how in thrall
    Lord Lancelot lay to love, who loved the Queen;
    We were alone – we thought no harm at all.

As we read on, our eyes met now and then,
    And to our cheeks the changing colour started,
    But just one moment overcame us – when

We read of the smile, desired of lips long-thwarted,
    Such smile, by such a lover kissed away,
    He that may never more from me be parted

Trembling all over, kissed my mouth. I say
    The book was Galleot, Galleot the complying
    Ribald who wrote; we read no more that day.'

While the one spirit thus spoke, the other's crying
    Wailed on me with a sound so lamentable,
    I swooned for pity like as I were dying,

And, as a dead man falling, down I fell.

Canto VI

The Story. *Dante now finds himself in the Third Circle, where the Gluttonous lie wallowing in the mire, drenched by perpetual rain and mauled by the three-headed dog Cerberus. After Virgil has quieted Cerberus by throwing earth into his jaws, Dante talks to the shade of Ciacco, a Florentine, who prophesies some of the disasters which are about to befall Florence, and tells him where he will find certain other of their fellow-citizens. Virgil tells Dante what the condition of the spirits will be, after the Last Judgment.*

When consciousness returned, which had shut close
    The doors of sense, leaving me stupefied
    For pity of those sad kinsfolk and their woes,

New sufferings and new sufferers, far and wide,
    Where'er I move, or turn myself, or strain
    My curious eyes, are seen on every side.

I am now in the Third Circle: that of rain –
    One ceaseless, heavy, cold, accursed quench,
    Whose law and nature vary never a grain;

Huge hailstones, sleet and snow, and turbid drench
    Of water sluice down through the darkened air,
    And the soaked earth gives off a putrid stench.

Cerberus, the cruel, misshapen monster, there
   Bays in his triple gullet and doglike growls
   Over the wallowing shades; his eyeballs glare

A bloodshot crimson, and his bearded jowls
   Are greasy and black; pot-bellied, talon-heeled,
   He clutches and flays and rips and rends the souls.

They howl in the rain like hounds; they try to shield
   One flank with the other; with many a twist and squirm,
   The impious wretches writhe in the filthy field.

When Cerberus spied us coming, the great Worm,
   He gaped his mouths with all their fangs a-gloat,
   Bristling and quivering till no limb stood firm.

At once my guide, spreading both hands wide out,
   Scooped up whole fistfuls of the miry ground
   And shot them swiftly into each craving throat.

And as a ravenous and barking hound
   Falls dumb the moment he gets his teeth on food,
   And worries and bolts with never a thought beyond,

So did those beastly muzzles of the rude
   Fiend Cerberus, who so yells on the souls, they're all
   Half deafened – or they would be, if they could.

Then o'er the shades whom the rain's heavy fall
   Beats down, we forward went; and our feet trod
   Their nothingness, which seems corporeal.

These all lay grovelling flat upon the sod;
    Only, as we went by, a single shade
    Sat suddenly up, seeing us pass that road.

'O thou that through this Hell of ours art led,
    Look if thou know me, since thou wast, for sure,'
    Said he, 'or ever I was unmade, made.'

Then I to him: 'Perchance thy torments sore
    Have changed thee out of knowledge – there's no
      trusting
    Sight, if I e'er set eyes on thee before.

But say, who art thou? brought by what ill lusting
    To such a pass and punishment as, meseems,
    Worse there may be, but nothing so disgusting?'

'Thy native city,' said he, 'where envy teems
    And swells so that already it brims the sack,
    Called me her own in the life where the light beams.

Ciacco you citizens nicknamed me – alack!
    Damnable gluttony was my soul's disease;
    See how I waste for it now in the rain's wrack.

And I, poor sinner, am not alone: all these
    Lie bound in the like penalty with me
    For the like offence.' And there he held his peace,

And I at once began: 'Thy misery
    Moves me to tears, Ciacco, and weighs me down.
    But tell me if thou canst, what end may be

In store for the people of our distracted town.
    Is there one just man left? And from what source
    To such foul head have these distempers grown?'

And he: 'Long time their strife will run its course,
    And come to bloodshed; the wood party thence
    Will drive the other out with brutal force;

But within three brief suns their confidence
    Will have a fall, and t'other faction rise
    By help of one who now sits on the fence;

And these will lord it long with arrogant eyes,
    Crushing their foes with heavy loads indeed,
    For all their bitter shame and outraged cries.

Two righteous men there are, whom none will heed;
    Three sparks from Hell – Avarice, Envy, Pride –
    In all men's bosoms sowed the fiery seed.'

His boding speech thus ended; so I cried:
    'Speak on, I beg thee! More, much more reveal!
    Tegghiaio, Farinata – how betide

Those worthy men? and Rusticucci's zeal?
    Arrigo, Mosca, and the rest as well
    Whose minds were still set on the public weal?

Where are they? Can I find them? Prithee tell –
   I am consumed with my desire to know –
   Feasting in Heaven, or poisoned here in Hell?'

He answered: 'With the blacker spirits below,
   Dragged to the depth by other crimes abhorred;
   There shalt thou see them, if so deep thou go.

But when to the sweet world thou art restored,
   Recall my name to living memory;
   I'll tell no more, nor speak another word.'

Therewith he squinted his straight gaze awry,
   Eyed me awhile, then, dropping down his head,
   Rolled over amid that sightless company.

Then spake my guide: 'He'll rouse no more,' he said,
   'Till the last loud angelic trumpet's sounding;
   For when the Enemy Power shall come arrayed

Each soul shall seek its own grave's mournful mounding,
   Put on once more its earthly flesh and feature,
   And hear the Doom eternally redounding.'

Thus with slow steps I and my gentle teacher,
   Over that filthy sludge of souls and snow,
   Passed on, touching a little upon the nature

Of the life to come. 'Master,' said I, 'this woe –
   Will it grow less, or still more fiercely burning
   With the Great Sentence, or remain just so?'

'Go to,' said he, 'hast thou forgot thy learning,
    Which hath it: The more perfect, the more keen,
    Whether for pleasure's or for pain's discerning?

Though true perfection never can be seen
    In these damned souls, they'll be more near
      complete
    After the Judgment than they yet have been.'

So, with more talk which I need not repeat,
    We followed the road that rings that circle round,
    Till on the next descent we set our feet;

There Pluto, the great enemy, we found.

Canto VII

The Story. *At the entrance to the Fourth Circle, the poets are opposed by Pluto, and Virgil is again obliged to use a 'word of power'. In this circle, the Hoarders and the Spendthrifts roll huge rocks against one another, and here Virgil explains the nature and working of Luck (or Fortune). Then, crossing the circle, they descend the cliff to the Marsh of Styx, which forms the Fifth Circle and contains the Wrathful. Skirting its edge, they reach the foot of a tower.*

'Papè Satan, papè Satan aleppe,'
    Pluto 'gan gabble with his clucking tongue;
    My all-wise, gentle guide, to me unhappy

Said hearteningly: 'Let no fears do thee wrong;
    He shall not stay thy journey down this steep;
    His powers, whate'er they be, are not so strong.'

Then, turning him, and letting his glance sweep
    O'er that bloat face: 'Peace, thou damned wolf!' said he,
    'Go, choke in thine own venom! To the deep,

Not without cause, we go. I say to thee,
    Thus it is willed on high, where Michaël
    Took vengeance on the proud adultery.'

Then, as the sails bellying in the wind's swell
   Tumble a-tangle at crack of the snapping mast,
   Even so to earth the savage monster fell;

And we to the Fourth Circle downward passed,
   Skirting a new stretch of the grim abyss
   Where all the ills of all the world are cast.

God's justice! Who shall tell the agonies,
   Heaped thick and new before my shuddering glance?
   Why must our guilt smite us with strokes like this?

As waves against the encountering waves advance
   Above Charybdis, clashing with toppling crest,
   So must the folk here dance and counter-dance.

More than elsewhere, I saw them thronged and pressed
   This side and that, yelling with all their might,
   And shoving each a great weight with his chest.

They bump together, and where they bump, wheel right
   Round, and return, trundling their loads again,
   Shouting: 'Why chuck away?' 'Why grab so tight?'

Then round the dismal ring they pant and strain
   Back on both sides to where they first began,
   Still as they go bawling their rude refrain;

And when they meet, then each re-treads his span,
   Half round the ring to joust in the other list;
   I felt quite shocked, and like a stricken man.

'Pray tell me, sir,' said I, 'all this – what is't?
    Who are these people? On our left I find
    Numberless tonsured heads; was each a priest?'

'In life,' said he, 'these were so squint of mind
    As in the handling of their wealth to use
    No moderation – none, in either kind;

That's plain, from their shrill yelpings of abuse
    At the ring's turn, where opposite degrees
    Of crime divide them into rival crews.

They whose pates boast no hairy canopies
    Are clerks – yea, popes and cardinals, in whom
    Covetousness hath made its masterpiece.'

'Why, sir,' said I, 'surely there must be some
    Faces I know in all this gang, thus brought
    By these defilements to a common doom.'

'Nay,' he replied, 'that is an empty thought;
    Living, their minds distinguished nothing; dead,
    They cannot be distinguished. In this sort

They'll butt and brawl for ever; when from bed
    The Last Trump wakes the body, these will be
    Raised with tight fists, and those stripped, hide and
        head.

Hoarding and squandering filched the bright world's
　　glee
　　Away, and set them to this tourney's shock,
　　Whose charms need no embroidered words from me.

See now, my son, the fine and fleeting mock
　　Of all those goods men wrangle for – the boon
　　That is delivered into the hand of Luck;

For all the gold that is beneath the moon;
　　Or ever was, could not avail to buy
　　Repose for one of these weary souls – not one.'

'Master, I would hear more of this,' said I;
　　'What is this Luck, whose talons take in hand
　　All life's good things that go so pleasantly?'

Then he: 'Ah, witless world! Behold the grand
　　Folly of ignorance! Make thine ear attendant
　　Now on my judgment of her, and understand.

He whose high wisdom's over all transcendent
　　Stretched forth the Heavens, and guiding spirits
　　　supplied,
　　So that each part to each part shines resplendent,

Spreading the light equal on every side;
　　Likewise for earthly splendours He saw fit
　　To ordain a general minister and guide,

By whom vain wealth, as time grew ripe for it,
    From race to race, from blood to blood, should pass,
    Far beyond hindrance of all human wit.

Wherefore some nations minish, some amass
    Great power, obedient to her subtle codes,
    Which are hidden, like the snake beneath the grass.

For her your science finds no measuring-rods;
    She in her realm provides, maintains, makes laws,
    And judges, as do in theirs the other gods.

Her permutations never know truce nor pause;
    Necessity lends her speed, so swift in fame
    Men come and go, and cause succeeds to cause.

Lo! this is she that hath so curst a name
    Even from those that should give praise to her –
    Luck, whom men senselessly revile and blame;

But she is blissful and she does not hear;
    She, with the other primal creatures, gay
    Tastes her own blessedness, and turns her sphere.

Come! to more piteous woes we must away;
    All stars that rose when I set out now sink,
    And the High Powers permit us no long stay.'

So to the further edge we crossed the rink,
    Hard by a bubbling spring which, rising there,
    Cuts its own cleft and pours on down the brink.

Darker than any perse its waters were,
    And keeping company with the ripples dim
    We made our way down by that eerie stair.

A marsh there is called Styx, which the sad stream
    Forms when it finds the end of its descent
    Under the grey, malignant rock-foot grim;

And I, staring about with eyes intent,
    Saw mud-stained figures in the mire beneath,
    Naked, with looks of savage discontent,

At fisticuffs – not with fists alone, but with
    Their heads and heels, and with their bodies too,
    And tearing each other piecemeal with their teeth.

'Son,' the kind master said, 'here may'st thou view
    The souls of those who yielded them to wrath;
    Further, I'd have thee know and hold for true

That others lie plunged deep in this vile broth,
    Whose sighs – see there, wherever one may look –
    Come bubbling up to the top and make it froth.

Bogged there they say: 'Sullen were we – we took
    No joy of the pleasant air, no joy of the good
    Sun; our hearts smouldered with a sulky smoke;

Sullen we lie here now in the black mud.'
    This hymn they gurgle in their throats, for whole
    Words they can nowise frame.' Thus we pursued

Our path round a wide arc of that ghast pool,
   Between the soggy marsh and arid shore,
   Still eyeing those who gulp the marish foul,

And reached at length the foot of a tall tower.

[. . .]

Canto X

The Story. *As the Poets are passing along beneath the city walls, Dante is hailed by Farinata from one of the burning tombs, and goes to speak to him. Their conversation is interrupted by Cavalcante dei Cavalcanti with a question about his son. Farinata prophesies Dante's exile and explains how the souls in Hell know nothing of the present, though they can remember the past and dimly foresee the future.*

Thus onward still, following a hidden track
    Between the city's ramparts and the fires,
    My master goes, and I go at his back.

'O sovran power, that through the impious gyres,'
    Said I, 'dost wheel me as thou deemest well,
    Speak to me, satisfy my keen desires.

Those that find here their fiery burial,
    May they be seen? for nothing seems concealed;
    The lids are raised, and none stands sentinel.'

And he: 'All these shall be shut fast and sealed
    When from Jehoshaphat they come anew,
    Bringing their bodies now left far afield.

And hereabouts lie buried, close in view,
   Epicure and his followers – they who hold
   That when the body dies the soul dies too.

Hence that demand thou choosest to unfold
   May here and now be fully satisfied,
   Likewise thy hidden wish, to me untold.'

'Alas,' said I, 'from thee I'd never hide
   One single thought, save that short speech is sweet,
   As thou hast warned me once or twice, dear guide.'

'O Tuscan, walking thus with words discreet
   Alive through the city of fire, be it good to thee
   To turn thee hither awhile, and stay thy feet.

Thy native accent proves thee manifestly
   Born of the land I vexed with so great harm –
   A noble land, and too much vext, maybe.'

This summons threw me into such alarm,
   Coming suddenly from a tomb, that in my dread
   I shrank up close against my escort's arm.

'Come, come, what art thou doing? Turn round,' he said;
   'That's Farinata – look! he's risen to sight,
   And thou canst view him all, from waist to head.'

Already my eyes were fixed on his; upright
   He had lifted him, strong-breasted, stony-fronted,
   Seeming to hold all Hell in deep despite;

And my good guide, with ready hands undaunted
   Thrusting me toward him through the tombs apace,
   Said: 'In thy speech precision is what's wanted.'

I reached the vault's foot, and he scanned my face
   A little while, and then said, with an air
   Almost contemptuous: 'What's thy name and race?'

Being anxious to obey, I did not care
   To make a mystery, but told all out;
   He raised his brows a trifle, saying: 'They were

Foes to me always, stubborn, fierce to flout
   Me and my house and party; I was quick
   To chase them, twice I put them to the rout.'

'Quite true; and by that same arithmetic,'
   Said I, 'they rallied all round and came back twice;
   Your side, it seems, have not yet learnt the trick.'

Just then, close by him, I saw slowly rise
   Another shadow, visible down to the chin;
   It had got to its knees, I think. It moved its eyes

Round about me, as though it sought to win
   Sight of some person in my company;
   At last, when all such hope lay quenched within,

It wept: 'If thy grand art has made thee free
   To walk at large in this blind prison of pain,
   Where is my son? why comes he not with thee?'

'I come not of myself,' I answered plain,
  'He that waits yonder leads me on this road,
  For whom, perhaps, your Guido felt disdain.'

The words he used, together with his mode
  Of torment, were sufficient to betray
  His name, as thus my pointed answer showed.

He leapt upright, crying: 'What? what dost thou say?
  He felt? why felt? are life and feeling o'er?
  Looks he no longer on the pleasant day?'

Then, seeing me hesitate awhile before
  I made reply, he let himself suddenly fall
  Backward again, and showed his face no more.

But that great-hearted spirit, at whose call
  I'd stayed my steps, his countenance did not move,
  Nor bent his neck, nor stirred his side at all.

'And if,' he spoke straight on where we broke off,
  'If they have missed the trick of it, I burn
  Less in this bed than with the thought thereof.

But thou, ere fifty times the light return
  To that queen's face who reigneth here below,
  Shalt find out just what that trick costs to learn.

But tell me why, as thou dost hope to go
  Back to the light, thy people make decrees
  So harsh against our house, and hate us so.'

'That field of havoc and bloody butcheries,'
   I answered him, 'when Arbia's stream ran red,
   Have filled our temple with these litanies.'

He sighed before he spoke, and shook his head:
   ' 'Faith, I was not alone there, nor had gone
   In with the rest without good cause,' he said;

'But when they made agreement, every one,
   To wipe out Florence, and I stood to plead
   Boldly for her – ay, there I was alone.'

'Now, so may rest come some time to your seed,'
   Said I, 'pray solve me this perplexity,
   Which ties my brains in a tight knot indeed.

It seems you can foresee and prophesy
   Events that time will bring, if I hear right,
   But with things present, you deal differently.'

'We see,' said he, 'like men who are dim of sight,
   Things that are distant from us; just so far
   We still have gleams of the All-Guider's light.

But when these things draw near, or when they are,
   Our intellect is void, and your world's state
   Unknown, save someone bring us news from there.

Hence thou wilt see that all we can await
   Is the stark death of knowledge in us, then
   When time's last hour shall shut the future's gate.'

At this my conscience smote me; I again
   Addressed him: 'Tell that fallen shade, I pray,
   His son still walks the world of living men;

If I was silent when he asked me, say
   'Twas only that my wits were in a worry,
   Snared by that error which you've swept away.'

And now my guide was calling me to hurry,
   Wherefore I urged the shade, with greater haste,
   To say who else was in that cemetery.

'I lie,' said he, 'with thousands; in this chest
   The second Frederick lies; our ranks include
   The Cardinal; I will not name the rest.'

He spoke, and sank; returning to where stood
   The ancient poet, I pondered what they meant,
   Those words which seemed to bode me little good.

Then he moved on, and later, as we went,
   'Why so distraught?' said he. I set to work
   Answering his question to his full content.

Sagely he bad me: 'See thou mind and mark
   Those adverse warnings; now to what I say' –
   And here he raised his finger – 'prithee, hark!

When thou shalt stand bathed in the glorious ray
   Of her whose blest eyes see all things complete
   Thou'lt learn the meaning of thy life's whole way.'

With that, leaving the wall, we turned our feet
   Towards the centre, by a path that ran
   Down to a vale, whose fumes rose high to greet

Our nostrils, even where the descent began.

Canto XI

The Story. While the Poets pause for a little on the brink of the descent to the Seventh Circle, Virgil explains to Dante the arrangement of Hell.

Where a great cliff fell sheer, its beetling brow
    Ringed with huge jagged rocks, we reached the
      brink
    O'erhanging the still ghastlier dens below;

And here so overpowering was the stink
    The deep Abyss threw off, that we withdrew
    Staggered, and for a screen were forced to shrink

Behind a massive vault where, plain to view,
    Stood writ: 'I hold Pope Anastasius,
    Lured by Photinus from the pathway true.'

'We'll wait awhile,' the master said, 'that thus
    Our senses may grow used to this vile scent,
    And after that, it will not trouble us.'

And I: 'But let's not lose the time so spent;
    Think now what compensation thou canst find.'
    'Surely,' he answered, 'such was my intent.

See now, my son: three narrowing circles wind
   Within these cliffs,' thus he took up the tale,
   'Each under each, like those we've left behind.

Damned spirits fill them all; thou canst not fail
   To know them at a glance, though, if I state
   How and for what they're here pent up in jail.

Of all malicious wrong that earns Heaven's hate
   The end is injury; all such ends are won
   Either by force or fraud. Both perpetrate

Evil to others; but since man alone
   Is capable of fraud, God hates that worst;
   The fraudulent lie lowest, then, and groan

Deepest. Of these three circles, all the first
   Holds violent men; but as threefold may be
   Their victims, in three rings they are dispersed.

God, self, and neighbour – against all these three
   Force may be used; either to injure them
   Or theirs, as I shall show convincingly.

Man on his neighbour may bring death or mayhem
   By force; or damage his chattels, house, and lands
   By harsh extortions, pillage, or fire and flame;

So murderers, men who are violent of their hands,
   Robbers and plunderers, all find chastisement
   In the first ring, disposed in various bands.

Against themselves men may be violent,
    And their own lives or their own goods destroy;
    So they in the second ring in vain repent

Who rob themselves of your world, or make a toy
    Of fortune, gambling and wasting away their purse,
    And turn to weeping what was meant for joy.

Those men do violence to God, who curse
    And in their hearts deny Him, or defame
    His bounty and His Natural Universe;

So the third ring sets its seal on the double shame
    Of Sodom and of Cahors, and on the speech
    Of the froward heart, dishonouring God's great name.

Fraud, which gnaws every conscience, may be a breach
    Of trust against the confiding, or deceive
    Such as repose no confidence; though each

Is fraud, the latter sort seems but to cleave
    The general bond of love and Nature's tie;
    So the second circle opens to receive

Hypocrites, flatterers, dealers in sorcery,
    Panders and cheats, and all such filthy stuff,
    With theft, and simony and barratry.

Fraud of the other sort forgets both love
    Of kind, and that love too whence is begot
    The special trust that's over and above;

So, in the smallest circle, that dark spot,
    Core of the universe and throne of Dis,
    The traitors lie; and their worm dieth not.'

'Master,' said I, 'how clear thy discourse is!
    It makes this gulf's arrangement plain as plain,
    With all its inmates; I quite follow this;

But tell me: all those others, whom the rain
    Beats, and the wind drives, and the sticky mire
    Bogs, and those brawlers with their shrill campaign

Why dwell not they in the city red with fire
    If to God's wrath they too are fallen a prey?
    Or if not, wherefore is their plight so dire?'

'What error has seduced thy reason, pray?'
    Said he, 'thou art not wont to be so dull;
    Or are thy wits woolgathering miles away?

Dost thou not mind the doctrine of thy school –
    Those pages where the *Ethics* tells of three
    Conditions contrary to Heaven's will and rule,

Incontinence, vice, and brute bestiality?
    And how incontinence offends God less
    Than the other two, and is less blameworthy?

If thou wilt think on what this teaching says,
    Bearing in mind what sort of sinners dwell
    Outside the city, and there endure distress,

Thou'lt see why they lie separate from these fell
    Spirits within, and why God's hammer-blow
    Of doom smites them with weight less terrible.'

'O Sun that healest all dim sight, thou so
    Dost charm me in resolving of my doubt,
    To be perplexed is pleasant as to know.

Just once again,' said I, 'turn thee about
    To where thou spak'st of usury as a crime
    Against God's bounty – ravel me that knot out.'

'Not in one place,' said he, 'but many a time
    Philosophy points out to who will learn,
    How Nature takes her course from the Sublime

Intellect and Its Art; note that; then turn
    The pages of thy *Physics*, and not far
    From the beginning, there shalt thou discern

How your Art, as it best can, follows her
    Like a pupil with his master; we may call
    This art of yours God's grandchild, as it were.

By Art and Nature, if thou well recall
    How Genesis begins, man ought to get
    His bread, and make prosperity for all.

But the usurer contrives a third way yet,
    And in herself and in her follower, Art,
    Scorns Nature, for his hope is elsewhere set.

Follow me now; I think we should depart;
  Horizon-high the twinkling Fishes swim,
  And the Wain's right over Caurus; we must start

Onward and downward, over the chasm's rim.'

[. . .]

Canto XIII

The Story. *The Poets enter a pathless Wood. Here Harpies sit shrieking among the withered trees, which enclose the souls of Suicides. Pier delle Vigne tells Dante his story, and also explains how these shades come to be changed into trees and what will happen to their bodies at the Last Day. The shades of two Profligates rush through the wood, pursued and torn by black hounds. Dante speaks to a bush containing the soul of a Florentine.*

Ere Nessus had regained the bank beyond,
    We'd pushed into a forest, where no mark
    Of any beaten path was to be found.

No green here, but discoloured leaves and dark,
    No tender shoots, but writhen and gnarled and
      tough,
    No fruit, but poison-galls on the withered bark.

Wild beasts, from tilth and pasture slinking off
    'Twixt Cecina and Corveto, never come
    To lurk in scrub so tangled or so rough.

There the foul Harpies nest and are at home,
    Who chased the Trojans from the Strophades
    With dismal outcry ominous of doom.

Wide-winged like birds and lady-faced are these,
   With feathered belly broad and claws of steel;
   And there they sit and shriek on the strange trees.

And the good master thus began: ' 'Twere well,
   Ere going further, thou shouldst understand,
   Thou'rt now in the second ring, and shalt be, till

Thou comest to the abominable sand.
   But now, look well, and see a thing whose telling
   Might kill my credit with thee out of hand.'

Already all round I heard a mournful wailing,
   But, seeing none to wail, I stopped short, blinking
   Bewilderedly, as though my wits were failing.

I think he must have thought that I was thinking
   That all these voices through the boles resounding
   Were those of folk who from our gaze hid shrinking,

Because he said: 'If from these boughs abounding
   Thou wilt pluck off one small and single spray,
   Thy thoughts will stagger at their own dumbfounding.'

So I put forth my hand a little way,
   And broke a branchlet from a thorn-tree tall;
   And the trunk cried out: 'Why tear my limbs away?'

Then it grew dark with blood, and the therewithal
   Cried out again: 'Why dost thou rend my bones?
   Breathes there no pity in thy breast at all?

We that are turned to trees were human once;
    Nay, thou shouldst tender a more pious hand
    Though we had been the souls of scorpions.'

As, when you burn one end of a green brand,
    Sap at the other oozes from the wood,
    Sizzling as the imprisoned airs expand,

So from that broken splint came words and blood
    At once: I dropped the twig, and like to one
    Rooted to the ground with terror, there I stood.

'O wounded soul,' my sage replied anon,
    'Might I have brought him straightway to believe
    The thing he'd read of in my verse alone,

Never had he lifted finger to mischieve
    Thee thus; but 'twas incredible; so I
    Prompted his deed, for which myself must grieve.

But tell him who thou wast, that he may try
    For some amends, to right thee with mankind
    When, by permission, he returns on high.'

To this the trunk made answer: 'Words so kind
    Tempt me to speech; nor take it in ill part
    If at some length I'm lured to speak my mind.

I am he that held both keys of Frederick's heart,
    To lock and to unlock; and well I knew
    To turn them with so exquisite an art,

I kept his counsel and let few men through;
   Loyal to my glorious charge did I remain,
   And sacrificed my sleep and my strength too

But that great harlot which can ne'er refrain
   From Caesar's household her adulterous eyes,
   The vice of kings' courts and their common bane,

Inflamed all hearts against me, and these likewise,
   Flaming, inflamed Augustus to distrust,
   Till my glad honours turned to obloquies.

So, in a scornful spirit of disgust,
   And thinking to escape from scorn by death,
   To my just self I made myself unjust;

But by these strange new roots my trunk beneath,
   Never to my most honourworthy lord,
   I swear to you, was I found false of faith;

And if to that bright world indeed restored
   One of you goes, oh, heal my memory,
   Which lies and bleeds from envy's venomed sword.'

He paused there; and the poet said to me:
   'While he is mute, let not this moment go,
   But speak, and ask what more seems good to thee.'

And I: 'Ask thou, whate'er thou think'st will do
   My hunger good and satisfy me well;
   I cannot ask, pity unhearts me so.'

Wherefore: 'So may this man prove liberal,'
    Thus he resumed, 'thine errand to perform,
    Imprisoned spirit, do thou be pleased to tell

How souls get cramped into this knotty form,
    And, if thou canst, if any shall do off
    These limbs one day and find release therefrom.'

At this the trunk blew hard, and the windy puff
    After this wise soon whistled into speech:
    'You shall be answered with brief words enough.

When the wild soul leaps from the body, which
    Its own mad violence forces it to quit,
    Minos dispatches it down to the seventh ditch.

It falls in the wood; no place is picked for it,
    But as chance carries it, there it falls to be,
    And where it falls, it sprouts like a corn of wheat,

And grows to a sapling, and thence to a wild tree;
    Then the Harpies feed on its leaves, and the sharp bite
    Gives agony, and a vent to agony.

We shall take our flight, when all souls take their flight,
    To seek our spoils, but not to be rearrayed,
    For the spoils of the spoiler cannot be his by right;

Here shall we drag them, to this gloomy glade;
    Here shall they hang, each body evermore
    Borne on the thorn of its own self-slaughtering shade.'

Thinking the trunk might wish to tell us more,
    We stood intent, when suddenly there came
      crashing
    On our astonished ears a wild uproar,

As the huntsman hears the boar and the chase dashing
    Down on his post like the noise of a hurricane,
    With trampling of beasts and all the branches
      smashing.

And lo! on the left of us came two that ran
    Naked and torn, with such a furious burst
    As snapped to flinders every forest fan.

'O death, come now, come quickly!' thus the first;
    And the second, finding himself outstripped in the
      rush,
    Cried: 'Lano, thy legs were not so nimble erst

At the jousts of Toppo.' So in the last push,
    His breath failing perhaps, he shot sidelong
    And made one group of himself and a thick bush.

And filling the woods behind them came a throng
    Of great black braches, fleet of foot and grim,
    And keen as greyhounds fresh-slipped from the
      thong;

They seized the skulker, and set their teeth in him,
    And rent him piecemeal, and away they went
    Carrying the wretched fragments limb by limb.

Then my guide drew me by the hand, and bent
   His steps to the poor bush, left mangled there,
   Gasping vain protests through each bleeding rent.

'O Jacomo,' it cried, 'of Sant' Andrea,
   Why make a screen of me? What was the good?
   Am I to blame for thy misspent career?'

Then said my gentle master when he stood
   Beside it: 'Who wast thou, that through such
     tattered
   Wounds sighest out thy grief mingled with blood?'

'O spirits, who come in time to see me battered
   Thus shamefully, and all my foliage torn,'
   It said, 'bring back the leaves that lie there scattered,

Gather them close beneath the shrub forlorn.
   My city was she that for the Baptist changed
   Her ancient patron, wherefore on her scorn

Still by his art he makes himself avenged;
   Yea, did not Arno's bridge even now retain
   Some image of the guardian she estranged,

Those citizens who built her walls again
   On the ashes left by Attila, had been baffled
   Wholly, and all their labour spent in vain;

I am one that made my own roof-tree my scaffold.'

Canto XIV

The Story. *In a desert of Burning Sand, under a rain of perpetual fire, Dante finds the Violent against God, Nature, and Art. The Violent against God lie supine, facing the Heaven which they insulted; among these is Capaneus, blasphemous and defiant in death as in life. The Poets pick their way carefully between the forest and the hot sand till they come to the edge of a boiling, red stream. Here Virgil explains the origin of all the rivers of Hell.*

Love of my native place with kind constraint
    Moving me, I brought back the scattered leaves
    To him whose voice already was grown faint;

Then on we went, to reach the bound which cleaves
    The second ring from the third, and saw appear
    A terrible art which justice here conceives.

I say, to make all this new matter clear,
    We reached a plain which spurns all foliage
    And every live plant from its surface sere.

The doleful wood garlands it like a hedge,
    As the sad moat garlands the wood around;
    And here we stayed our steps 'twixt edge and edge.

An arid, close-packed sand, in fashion found
  Not otherwise than that which once was trod
  By Cato's marching feet, such was the ground.

Fearful indeed art thou, vengeance of God!
  He that now reads what mine own eyes with awe
  Plainly beheld, well may he dread thy rod!

Great herds of naked spirits here I saw,
  Who all most wretchedly bewailed their lot,
  Seeming subjected to a diverse law.

Some on the ground lay supine in one spot,
  And some upon their hunkers squatted low,
  Others roamed ceaselessly and rested not;

Most numerous were the rovers to-and-fro;
  Of those that lay, the numbers were more small,
  But much the loudest were their cries of woe.

And slowly, slowly dropping over all
  The sand, there drifted down huge flakes of fire,
  As Alpine snows in windless weather fall.

Like as Alexander, in those torrider
  Regions of Ind, saw flaming fireballs shed
  Over his host, floating to earth entire,

So that his men and he took pains to tread
  The soil, trampling the blaze out with their feet,
  Since it was easier quenched before it spread,

Even so rained down the everlasting heat,
    And, as steel kindles tinder, kindled the sands,
    Redoubling pain; nor ever ceased the beat

And restless dance of miserable hands,
    Flapping away, now this side and now that,
    The raw smart of the still-fresh-biting brands.

I thus began: 'Master, strong to frustrate
    All hostile things, save only indeed those grim
    Fiends who opposed our entrance at the gate,

Who is the shade that lies, mighty of limb,
    Contorted and contemptuous, scorning the flame,
    So that the rain seems not to ripen him?'

But he himself, soon as he heard me frame
    This question to my guide about him, cried:
    'That which in life I was, in death I am.

Though Jove tire out his armourer, who supplied
    His wrathful hand with the sharp thunder-stone
    That in my last day smote me through the side;

Though he tire all the rest out, one by one,
    In Mongibel's black stithy, and break them quite,
    Crying, "To aid! Vulcan, lay on, lay on!"

As once before he cried at Phlegra's fight;
    Yea, though he crush me with his omnipotence,
    No merry vengeance shall his heart delight.'

Then my guide spoke out with a vehemence
    Such as I never had heard him use before:
    'O Capaneus, since thy proud insolence

Will not be quenched, thy pains shall be the more;
    No torment save thine own hot rage could be
    A fitting cautery to thy rabid sore.'

Then said with milder mouth, turning to me:
    'This was one of the seven kings who pressed
    The siege of Thebes; he held, and seemingly

Still holds, God light, and flouts Him with a jest;
    Yet, as I told him, his mad mouthings make
    A proper brooch for such a brazen breast.

Now follow me, and look to it that thou take
    No step upon the burning sand, but keep
    Thy feet close back against the woodland brake.'

Silent we came where, from that forest deep,
    A little brook poured forth a bubbling jet
    Whose horrid redness makes my flesh still creep.

It was like that stream of the Bulicame, set
    Apart and shared by the women of the town;
    And straight out over the sand ran the rivulet.

Its bed, and both its shelving banks, and the crown
    Of the margins left and right, were turned to stone;
    Which made me think that here our path led down.

'Of all the marvels I as yet have shown
 Thine eyes, since first we entered by that door
 Of which the threshold is denied to none,

Nothing we've seen deserves thy wonder more
 Than this small stream which, flowing centreward,
 Puts out all flames above its either shore.'

Thus said my guide; whom I at once implored,
 Since he'd so whet my appetite to taste
 His food, immediately to spread the board.

'Far off amid the sea there lies a waste
 Country,' said he, 'called Crete, beneath whose
  king,
 Once on a long-lost time, the world was chaste.

A mount is there, named Ida; many a spring
 Laughed through its ferns of yore and the valleys
  smiled
 Forsaken now, like some old, mouldering thing.

There Rhea once found safe cradling for her child,
 And to hide his cries, lest danger come to pass,
 Let fill the hills with Corybant clamours wild.

A great old man stands under the mountain's mass;
 Toward Damietta he keeps his shoulders holden,
 And he looks on Rome as though on a looking-glass.

He towers erect, and his head is purely golden,
    Of the silver fine his breast and arms and hands,
    Of brass down to the cleft his trunk is moulden,

And thence to the ground his legs are iron bands,
    Save that the right foot's baked of the earthen clay,
    And that is the foot upon which he chiefly stands.

All but the gold is cracked, and from the splay
    Of that great rift run tears gathering and dripping,
    Till out through the cavern floor they wear their
      way

Into this vale, from rock to rock down-dipping,
    Making Acheron, Styx and Phlegethon; then they take
    Their downward course, by this strait conduit
      slipping,

To where there is no more downward; there they
      make
    Cocytus; and what that's like I need not tell;
    For thine own eyes shall look on Cocytus lake.'

Then I to him: 'But, Master, if this rill
    Flows from our world, why is it only found
    Here on this bank, nor elsewhere visible?'

And he to me: 'Thou knowest, the place is round;
    Though thou hast come a good long way, 'tis true,
    Still wheeling leftward toward the Pit's profound,

Thou hast not yet turned the full circle through;
   So why put on such a bewildered air
   If now and then we come upon something new?'

And I again: 'Where's Lethe, sir? and where
   Is Phlegethon? The first thou leav'st aside,
   Tracing the second to that water there.'

'Thy questions all delight me,' he replied,
   'But for the one – thyself canst answer it:
   Think of the boiling of the blood-red tide.

And Lethe thou shalt see, far from this Pit,
   Where go the souls to wash them in its flood,
   Their guilt purged off, their penitence complete.'

He added: 'Come; it's time to leave the wood;
   See that thou follow closely where I tread;
   The margins burn not, they shall make our road,

And all the fires are quenched there overhead.'

[. . .]

Canto XVIII

The Story. *Dante now finds himself in the Eighth Circle (Malbowges), which is divided into ten trenches (bowges) containing those who committed Malicious Frauds upon mankind in general. The Poets walk along the edge of the First Bowge, where Panders and Seducers run, in opposite directions, scourged by demons; and here Dante talks with Venedico Caccianemico of Bologna. As they cross the bridge over the bowge, they see the shade of Jason. Then they go on to the bridge over the Second Bowge, where they see Thaïs, and Dante converses with another of the Flatterers who are here plunged in filth.*

There is in Hell a region that is called
   Malbowges; it is all of iron-grey stone,
   Like the huge barrier-rock with which it's walled.

Plumb in the middle of the dreadful cone
   There yawns a well, exceeding deep and wide,
   Whose form and fashion shall be told anon.

That which remains, then, of the foul Pit's side,
   Between the well and the foot of the craggy steep,
   Is a narrowing round, which ten great chasms divide.

As one may see the girding fosses deep
    Dug to defend a stronghold from the foe,
    Trench within trench about the castle-keep,

Such was the image here; and as men throw
    Their bridges outward from the fortress-wall,
    Crossing each moat to the far bank, just so

From the rock's base spring cliffs, spanning the fall
    Of dyke and ditch, to the central well, whose rim
    Cuts short their passage and unites them all.

When Geryon shook us off, 'twas in this grim
    Place that we found us; and the poet then
    Turned to the left, and I moved after him.

There, on our right, more anguished shades of men,
    New tortures and new torturers, I espied,
    Cramming the depth of this first bowge of ten.

In the bottom were naked sinners, who, our side
    The middle, moved to face us; on the other,
    Along with us, though with a swifter stride.

Just so the Romans, because of the great smother
    Of the Jubilee crowds, have thought of a good
        device
    For controlling the bridge, to make the traffic
        smoother,

So that on one side all must have their eyes
    On the Castle, and go to St Peter's; while all the
      throng
    On the other, towards the Mount moves
      contrariwise.

I saw horned fiends with heavy whips and strong
    Posted each side along the dismal rock,
    Who scourged their backs, and drove them on
      headlong.

Hey! how they made them skip at the first shock!
    How brisk they were to lift their legs and prance!
    Nobody stayed for the second or third stroke.

And as I was going, one of them caught my glance,
    And I promptly said to myself: 'How now! who's he?
    Somewhere or other I've seen that countenance.'

I stopped short, figuring out who this might be;
    And my good lord stopped too; then let me go
    Back a short way, to follow him and see.

The whipped shade hung his head, trying not to show
    His face; but little good he got thereby,
    For: 'Hey, there! thou whose eyes are bent so low,

Thy name's Venedico – or thy features lie –
    Caccianemico, and I know thee well;
    What wormwood pickled such a rod,' said I,

'To scrub thy back?' And he: 'I would not tell,
    But for that voice of thine; those accents clear
    Remind me of the old life, and compel

My answer. I am the man who sold the fair
    Ghisola to the Marchese's lust; that's fact,
    However they tell the ugly tale up there.

I'm not alone here from Bologna; packed
    The place is with us; one could scarcely find
    More tongues saying "Yep" for "Yes" in all the tract

'Twixt Reno and Savena. Art inclined
    To call for proof? What witness need I join
    To the known witness of our covetous mind?'

And one of the fiends caught him a crack on the loin
    With the lash, even as he spoke, crying: 'Away,
    Pander! there are no women here to coin!'

So to my escort I retraced my way,
    And soon we came, a few steps further wending,
    To where a great spur sprang from the barrier grey.

This we climbed lightly, and, right-handed bending,
    Crossed its rough crest, departing from that rout
    Of shades who run their circuits never-ending.

But, coming above the part that's tunnelled out
    To let the flogged pass under, 'Stay,' said he;
    'Let those who go the other way about

Strike on thine eyes; just now thou couldst not see
 Their faces, as we passed along the verge,
 For they were travelling the same road as we.'

So from that ancient bridge we watched the surge
 Sweep on towards us of the wretched train
 On the farther side, chased likewise by the scourge.

'Look who comes here,' my good guide said again
 Without my asking, 'that great spirit of old,
 Who will not shed one tear for all his pain.

Is he not still right royal to behold?
 That's Jason, who by valour and by guile
 Bore from the Colchian strand the fleece of gold.

He took his way past Lemnos, where, short while
 Before, the pitiless bold women achieved
 The death of all the menfolk of their isle;

And there the young Hypsipyle received
 Tokens and fair false words, till, snared and shaken,
 She who deceived her fellows was deceived;

And there he left her, childing and forsaken;
 For those deceits he's sentenced to these woes,
 And for Medea too revenge is taken.

And with him every like deceiver goes.
 Suffice thee so much knowledge of this ditch
 And those whom its devouring jaws enclose.'

Already we'd come to where the narrow ridge
  Crosses the second bank, and makes of it
  An abutment for the arch of the next bridge.

Here we heard people in the farther pit
  Make a loud whimpering noise, and heard them
    cough,
  And slap themselves with their hands, and snuffle
    and spit.

The banks were crusted with foul scum, thrown off
  By the fume, and caking there, till nose and eye
  Were vanquished with sight and reek of the noisome
    stuff.

So deep the trench, that one could not espy
  Its bed save from the topmost cliff, which makes
  The keystone of the arch. We climbed; and I,

Thence peering down, saw people in the lake's
  Foul bottom, plunged in dung, the which appeared
  Like human ordure running from a jakes.

Searching its depths, I there made out a smeared
  Head – whether clerk or lay was hard to tell,
  It was so thickly plastered with the merd.

'Why stand there gloating?' he began to yell,
  'Why stare at me more than the other scum?'
  'Because,' said I, 'if I remember well,

I've seen thy face, dry-headed, up at home;
  Thou art Alessio Interminei, late
  Of Lucca – so, more eagerly than on some,

I look on thee.' He beat his pumpkin pate,
  And said: 'The flatteries I spewed out apace
  With tireless tongue have sunk me to this state.'

Then said my guide: 'Before we leave the place,
  Lean out a little further, that with full
  And perfect clearness thou may'st see the face

Of that uncleanly and dishevelled trull
  Scratching with filthy nails, alternately
  Standing upright and crouching in the pool.

That is the harlot Thaïs. "To what degree,"
  Her leman asked, "have I earned thanks, my love?"
  "O, to a very miracle," said she.

And having seen this, we have seen enough.'

[. . .]

Canto XX

The Story. *In the Fourth Bowge of the Eighth Circle Dante sees the Sorcerers, whose heads are twisted so that they can only look behind them, and who are therefore compelled to walk backwards. Virgil tells him about the origin of Mantua. The moon is setting as the Poets leave the bowge.*

New punishments behoves me sing in this
   Twentieth canto of my first canticle,
   Which tells of spirits sunk in the Abyss.

I now stood ready to observe the full
   Extent of the new chasm thus laid bare,
   Drenched as it was in tears most miserable.

Through the round vale I saw folk drawing near,
   Weeping and silent, and at such slow pace
   As Litany processions keep, up here.

And presently, when I had dropped my gaze
   Lower than the head, I saw them strangely wried
   'Twixt collar-bone and chin, so that the face

Of each was turned towards his own backside,
   And backwards must they needs creep with their feet,
   All power of looking forward being denied.

Perhaps some kind of paralytic fit
    Could twist men so – such cases may have been;
    I never saw it, nor can I credit it;

And, Reader, so God give thee grace to glean
    Profit of my book, think if I could be left
    Dry-eyed, when close before me I had seen

Our image so distorted, so bereft
    Of dignity, that their eyes' brimming pools
    Spilled down to bathe the buttocks at the cleft.

Truly I wept, leaned on the pinnacles
    Of the hard rock; until my guide said, 'Why!
    And art thou too like all the other fools?

Here pity, or here piety, must die
    If the other lives; who's wickeder than one
    That's agonised by God's high equity?

Lift up, lift up thy head, and look upon
    Him for whom once the earth gaped wide, before
    The Thebans' eyes: "Whither wilt thou begone,

Amphiaraüs? Why leavest thou the war?"
    They cried; but he rushed down, and never stayed
    Till he reached Minos, that o'er such hath power.

See how he makes a breast of 's shoulder-blade!
    Because he tried to see too far ahead,
    He now looks backward and goes retrograde.

And lo you there Tiresias, who shed
   His proper shape and altered every limb,
   Changing his manhood for a womanhead,

So that he needs must smite the second time
   His wand upon the twin and tangled snakes
   To get his cock-feathers restored to him.

Aruns behind his breast back-forward makes;
   In Luna's mountains, at whose foot the knave
   Who dwells down in Carrara hoes and rakes,

He 'mid the white bright marbles had his cave;
   There lived, and there looked out, with nought to
     screen
   His view of starry Heaven and ocean wave.

And she that veils her breasts, by thee unseen,
   With her loose locks, and, viewed from where we
     stand,
   Has on the far side all her hairy skin

Was Manto, she that searched through many a land
   Ere settling in my birthplace; that's a tale
   I'd like to tell – brief patience, then, command.

After her father passed beyond life's pale,
   When Bacchus' city lay in bondage thralled,
   Long years she wandered up hill and down dale.

High in fair Italy, where Almayn's walled
   By the Alps above the Tyrol, lies and dreams
   At the mountain's foot a lake, Benaco called;

For the water here of over a thousand streams,
   Meseems, that lave Mount Apennine, running apace
   'Twixt Garda and Val Camonica, spreads and brims

To a mere; and there in the midst of it lies a place
   That the bishop of Verona, and those of Trent
   And Brescia, if they passed that way, might bless.

Peschiera sits at the circling shore's descent,
   'Gainst Bergamese and Brescians built for cover,
   A goodly keep; there all the effluent

Benaco's bosom cannot hold, spills over,
   Slipping and lipping down, and sliding so
   Through verdant meads, a river and a rover –

Benaco called no more, but Mincio,
   From where the water first sets head to run,
   Down to Governo, where it joins the Po.

It finds a level, ere half its course is done,
   And there stagnates and spreads to a marshy fen,
   Rank and unwholesome in the summer sun.

Passing that road, the cruel witch-maiden
   Found in the marsh firm tracts of land, which lay
   Untilled and uninhabited of men;

There, shunning human contact, did she stay
   With her familiar household; there she plied
   Her arts; there lived; there left her empty clay.

After, the scattered folk from far and wide
   Drew to the spot, which lay defensibly,
   Being girded by the swamp on every side.

O'er those dead bones they built their city, to be
   For her sake named that chose the place out thus,
   Mantua, with no further augury.

Far more than now it once was populous,
   Ere Casalodi's folly fell to the sword
   Of Pinamonte, who was treacherous.

I charge thee then, if stories go abroad,
   Other than this, of how my city grew,
   Let no such lying tales the truth defraud.'

'Master, for me thy teaching is so true,
   And so compels belief, all other tales,'
   Said I, 'were dust and ash compared thereto.

But tell me of this great crowd that yonder trails,
   If any worthy of note be now in sight;
   My mind harks back to that before all else.'

He answered: 'He whose chin-beard shows so white
   On his brown shoulders was a memorable
   Augur in Greece, what time the land was quite

Emptied of males, so that you'd scarce be able
   To find a cradling boy; he set the time,
   With Calchas, for the cutting of the first cable;

Eurpylus his name; and my sublime
   Tragedy sings him somewhere – thou'lt recall
   The place, that hast by heart the whole long rhyme.

That other there, who looks so lean and small
   In the flanks, was Michael Scott, who verily
   Knew every trick of the art magical.

Lo! Guy Bonatti; lo! Asdente – he
   May well wish now that he had stuck to his last,
   But he repents too late; and yonder see

The witch-wives, miserable women who cast
   Needle and spindle and shuttle away for skill
   With mommets and philtres; there they all go past.

But come! Cain with his thorn-bush strides the sill
   Of the two hemispheres; his lantern now
   Already dips to the wave below Seville;

And yesternight the moon was full, as thou
   Shouldst well remember, for throughout thy stay
   In the deep wood she harmed thee not, I trow.'

Thus he; and while he spake we went our way.

[. . .]

Canto XXVI

The Story. Dante, with bitter irony, reproaches Florence. The Poets climb up and along the rugged spur to the arch of the next bridge, from which they see the Counsellors of Fraud moving along the floor of the Eighth Bowge, each wrapped in a tall flame. Virgil stops the twin-flame which contains the souls of Ulysses and Diomede, and compels Ulysses to tell the story of his last voyage.

Florence, rejoice, because thy soaring fame
    Beats its broad wings across both land and sea,
    And all the deep of Hell rings with thy name!

Five of thy noble townsmen did I see
    Among the thieves; which makes me blush anew,
    And mighty little honour it does to thee.

But if toward the morning men dream true,
    Thou must ere long abide the bitter boon
    That Prato craves for thee, and others too;

Nay, were't already here, 'twere none too soon;
    Let come what must come, quickly – I shall find
    The burden heavier as the years roll on.

We left that place; and by the stones that bind
   The brink, which made the stair for our descent,
   My guide climbed back, and drew me up behind.

So on our solitary way we went,
   Up crags, up boulders, where the foot in vain
   Might seek to speed, unless the hand were lent.

I sorrowed then; I sorrow now again,
   Pondering the things I saw, and curb my hot
   Spirit with an unwontedly strong rein

For fear it run where virtue guide it not,
   Lest, if kind star or greater grace have blest
   Me with good gifts, I mar my own fair lot.

Now, thickly clustered, – as the peasant at rest
   On some hill-side, when he whose rays illume
   The world conceals his burning countenance least,

What time the flies go and mosquitoes come,
   Looks down the vale and sees the fire-flies sprinkling
   Fields where he tills or brings the vintage home –

So thick and bright I saw the eighth moat twinkling
   With wandering fires, soon as the arching road
   Laid bare the bottom of the deep rock-wrinkling.

Such as the chariot of Elijah showed
   When he the bears avenged beheld it rise,
   And straight to Heaven the rearing steeds upstrode,

For he could not so follow it with his eyes
　　But that at last it seemed a bodiless fire
　　Like a little shining cloud high in the skies,

So through that gulf moved every flaming spire;
　　For though none shows the theft, each, like a thief,
　　Conceals a pilfered sinner. To admire,

I craned so tip-toe from the bridge, that if
　　I had not clutched a rock I'd have gone over,
　　Needing no push to send me down the cliff.

Seeing me thus intently lean and hover,
　　My guide said: 'In those flames the spirits go
　　Shrouded, with their own torment for their cover.'

'Now thou hast told me, sir,' said I, 'I know
　　The truth for sure; but I'd already guessed,
　　And meant to ask – thinking it must be so –

Who walks in that tall fire cleft at the crest
　　As though it crowned the pyre where those great foes,
　　His brother and Eteocles, were placed?'

'Tormented there,' said he, 'Ulysses goes
　　With Diomede, for as they ran one course,
　　Sharing their wrath, they share the avenging throes.

In fire they mourn the trickery of the horse,
　　That opened up the gates through which the high
　　Seed of the Romans issued forth perforce;

There mourn the cheat by which betrayed to die
    Deïdamia wails Achilles still;
    And the Palladium is avenged thereby.'

Then I: 'O Master! if these sparks have skill
    To speak, I pray, and re-pray that each prayer
    May count with thee for prayers innumerable,

Deny me not to tarry a moment here
    Until the horned flame come: how much I long
    And lean to it I think thee well aware.'

And he to me: 'That wish is nowise wrong,
    But worthy of high praise; gladly indeed
    I grant it; but do thou refrain thy tongue

And let me speak to them; for I can read
    The question in thy mind; and they, being Greek,
    Haply might scorn thy speech and pay no heed.'

So, when by time and place the twin-fire peak,
    As to my guide seemed fitting, had come on,
    In this form conjuring it, I heard him speak:

'You that within one flame go two as one,
    By whatsoever I merited once of you,
    By whatsoever I merited under the sun

When I sang the high songs, whether little or great my
    due,
    Stand; and let one of you say what distant bourne,
    When he voyaged to loss and death, he voyaged
      unto.'

Then of that age-old fire the loftier horn
    Began to mutter and move, as a wavering flame
    Wrestles against the wind and is over-worn;

And, like a speaking tongue vibrant to frame
    Language, the tip of it flickering to and fro
    Threw out a voice and answered: 'When I came

From Circe at last, who would not let me go,
    But twelve months near Caieta hindered me
    Before Aeneas ever named it so,

No tenderness for my son, nor piety
    To my old father, nor the wedded love
    That should have comforted Penelope

Could conquer in me the restless itch to rove
    And rummage through the world exploring it,
    All human worth and wickedness to prove.

So on the deep and open sea I set
    Forth, with a single ship and that small band
    Of comrades that had never left me yet,

Far as Morocco, far as Spain I scanned
   Both shores; I saw the island of the Sardi,
   And all that sea, and every wave-girt land.

I and my fellows were grown old and tardy
   Or ere we made the straits where Hercules
   Set up his marks, that none should prove so hardy

To venture the uncharted distances;
   Ceuta I'd left to larboard, sailing by,
   Seville I now left in the starboard seas.

"Brothers," said I, "that have come valiantly
   Through hundred thousand jeopardies undergone
   To reach the West, you will not now deny

To this last little vigil left to run
   Of feeling life, the new experience
   Of the uninhabited world behind the sun.

Think of your breed; for brutish ignorance
   Your mettle was not made; you were made men,
   To follow after knowledge and excellence."

My little speech made every one so keen
   To forge ahead, that even if I'd tried
   I hardly think I could have held them in.

So, with our poop shouldering the dawn, we plied,
   Making our oars wings to the witless flight,
   And steadily gaining on the larboard side.

Already the other pole was up by night
   With all its stars, and ours had sunk so low,
   It rose no more from the ocean-floor to sight;

Five times we had seen the light kindle and grow
   Beneath the moon, and five times wane away,
   Since to the deep we had set course to go,

When at long last hove up a mountain, grey
   With distance, and so lofty and so steep,
   I never had seen the like on any day.

Then we rejoiced; but soon we had to weep,
   For out of the unknown land there blew foul
      weather,
   And a whirlwind struck the forepart of the ship;

And three times round she went in a roaring smother
   With all the waters; at the fourth, the poop
   Rose, and the prow went down, as pleased Another,

And over our heads the hollow seas closed up.'

[. . .]

Canto XXVIII

The Story. *From the bridge over the Ninth Bowge the Poets look down upon the Sowers of Discord, who are continually smitten asunder by a Demon with a sword. Dante is addressed by Mahomet and Pier da Medicina, who send messages of warning to people on earth. He sees Curio and Mosca, and finally Bertrand de Born.*

Who, though with words unshackled from the rhymes,
   Could yet tell full the tale of wounds and blood
   Now shown me, let him try ten thousand times?

Truly all tongues would fail, for neither could
   The mind avail, nor any speech be found
   For things not to be named nor understood.

If in one single place were gathered round
   All those whose life-blood in the days of yore
   Made outcry from Apulia's fateful ground,

Victims of Trojan frays, and that long war
   Whose spoil was heaped so high with rings of gold,
   As Livy tells, who errs not; those that bore

The hammering brunt of battle, being bold
   'Gainst Robert Guiscard to make stand on stand;
   And they whose bones still whiten in the mould

Of Ceperan', where all the Apulian band
   Turned traitors, and on Tagliacozzo's field
   Won by old Alard, weaponless and outmanned;

If each should show his bleeding limbs unhealed,
   Pierced, lopt and maimed, 'twere nothing, nothing
     whatever
   To that ghast sight in the ninth bowge revealed.

No cask stove in by cant or middle ever
   So gaped as one I saw there, from the chin
   Down to the fart-hole split as by a cleaver.

His tripes hung by his heels; the pluck and spleen
   Showed with the liver and the sordid sack
   That turns to dung the food it swallows in.

I stood and stared; he saw me and stared back;
   Then with his hands wrenched open his own
     breast,
   Crying: 'See how I rend myself! what rack

Mangles Mahomet! Weeping without rest
   Ali before me goes, his whole face slit
   By one great stroke upward from chin to crest.

All these whom thou beholdest in the pit
    Were sowers of scandal, sowers of schism abroad
    While they yet lived; therefore they now go split.

Back yonder stands a fiend, by whom we're scored
    Thus cruelly; and over and over again
    He puts us to the edge of the sharp sword

As we crawl through our bitter round of pain;
    For ere we come before him to be bruised
    Anew, the gashed flesh reunites its grain.

But who art thou that dalliest there bemused
    Up on the rock-spur – doubtless to delay
    Going to thy pangs self-judged and self-accused?'

'Nor dead as yet, nor brought here as a prey
    To torment by his guilt,' my master said,
    'But to gain full experience of the Way

He comes; wherefore behoves him to be led –
    And this is true as that I speak to thee –
    Gyre after gyre through Hell, by me who am dead.'

And, hearing him, stock-still to look on me
    Souls by the hundred stood in the valley of stone,
    And in amaze forgot their agony.

'Well, go then, thou that shalt behold the sun
    Belike ere long – let Fra Dolcino know,
    Unless he is in haste to follow me down,

He must well arm himself against the snow
    With victuals, lest the Novarese starve him out,
    Who else might find him hard to overthrow.'

Thus unto me Mahomet, with one foot
    Lifted to leave us; having said, he straight
    Stretched it to earth and went his dreary route.

Then one with gullet pierced and nose shorn flat
    Off to the very eyebrows, and who bare
    Only a single ear upon his pate,

Having remained with all the rest to stare,
    Before the rest opened his weasand now,
    Which outwardly ran crimson everywhere,

And said: 'O thou whom guilt condemns not, thou
    Whom I have seen up there in Italy
    Unless some likeness written in thy brow

Deceives me; if thou e'er return to see
    Once more the lovely plain that slopes between
    Vercelli and Marcabò, then think of me,

Of Pier da Medicina; and tell those twain,
    Ser Guido and Angiolello, Fano's best,
    That, if our foresight here be not all vain,

They'll be flung overboard and drowned, in the unblest
    Passage near La Cattolica, by the embargo
    Laid on their lives at a false lord's behest.

Neptune ne'er saw so foul a crime, such cargo
 Of wickedness 'twixt Cyprus and Majorca
 Ne'er passed, no pirate-crew, no men of Argo

Could show the like. That one-eyed mischief-worker
 Whose land there's one here with me in this vale
 Wishes he'd never seen, that smooth-tongued talker

Shall lure them to a parley, and when they sail
 Deal so with them that they shall have no need
 Of vow or prayer against Focara's gale.'

Then I to him: 'Tell me, so may I speed
 Thy message up to the world as thou dost seek,
 Who's he whose eyes brought him that bitter meed?'

At once he laid his hand upon the cheek
 Of a fellow-shade, and pulled his jaws apart,
 Saying: 'Look! this is he; he cannot speak.

This outcast quenched the doubt in Caesar's heart:
 "To men prepared delays are dangerous";
 Thus he gave sign for civil strife to start.'

O how deject to me, how dolorous
 Seemed Curio, with his tongue hacked from his throat,
 He that of speech was so adventurous!

And one that had both hands cut off upsmote
 The bloody stumps through the thick air and black,
 Sprinkling his face with many a filthy clot,

And cried: 'Think, too, on Mosca, Mosca alack!
   Who said: "What's done is ended," and thereby
   For Tuscany sowed seed of ruin and wrack.'

'And death to all thy kindred,' added I;
   Whereat, heaping despair upon despair,
   He fled, like one made mad with misery.

But I remained to watch the throng, and there
   I saw a thing I'd hesitate to tell
   Without more proof – indeed, I should not dare,

Did not a blameless conscience stead me well –
   That trusty squire that harnesses a man
   In his own virtue like a coat of mail.

Truly I saw – it seems to me I can
   See still – I saw a headless trunk that sped
   Running towards me as the others ran;

And by the hair it held the severed head
   Swung, as one swings a lantern, in its hand;
   And that caught sight of us: 'Ay me!' it said.

Itself was its own lamp, you understand,
   And two in one and one in two it was,
   But how – He only knows who thus ordained!

And when it reached our bridge, I saw it toss
   Arm up and head together, with design
   To bring the words it uttered near to us;

Which were: 'O breathing soul, brought here to win
   Sight of the dead, behold this grievous thing,
   See if there be any sorrow like to mine.

And know, if news of me thou seek to bring
   Yonder, Bertrand de Born am I, whose fell
   Counsel, warping the mind of the Young King,

Like Absalom with David, made rebel
   Son against father, father against son,
   Deadly as the malice of Achitophel.

Because I sundered those that should be one,
   I'm doomed, woe worth the day! to bear my brain
   Cleft from the trunk whence all its life should run;

Thus is my measure measured to me again.'

[. . .]

Canto XXX

The Story. *The shades of Myrrha and Gianni Schicchi are pointed out by Griffolino. Dante becomes intent upon a quarrel between Adam of Brescia and Sinon of Troy, and earns a memorable rebuke from Virgil.*

When Juno was incensed for Semele,
  And wreaking vengeance on the Theban race,
  As her sharp strokes had shown repeatedly,

So fierce a madness seized on Athamas
  That, seeing his wife go with her two young sons
  One on each arm: 'Spread nets, nets at the pass,

We'll take the lioness and the whelps at once!'
  He roared aloud; then, grasping in his wild
  And pitiless clutch one of those little ones,

Baby Learchus, as he crowed and smiled,
  He whirled him round and dashed him on a stone;
  She fled, and drowned herself with the other child.

And when, by Fortune's hostile hand o'erthrown,
  The towering pride of Troy fell to the ground,
  Kingdom and king together ruining down,

Sad Hecuba, forlorn and captive bound,
    After she'd seen Polyxena lie slain,
    After, poor hapless mother, she had found

Polydorus dead by the seashore, fell insane
    And howled like a dog, so fearfully distraught
    Was she, so wrenched out of her mind with pain.

Yet Theban or Trojan furies never wrought
    Such cruel frenzy, even in the maddened breast
    Of a brute, still less in any of human sort,

As I saw in two shades, naked, pale, possessed,
    Who ran, like a rutting boar that has made escape
    From the sty, biting and savaging all the rest.

One of them fell on Capocchio, catching his nape
    In its teeth, and dragging him prostrate, so that it made
    His belly on the rough rock-bottom scour and scrape.

The Aretine, left trembling, turned dismayed
    To me: 'That's Gianni Schicchi, that hell-hound there;
    He's rabid, he bites whatever he sees,' he said.

'So may thou 'scape the other's teeth, declare
    Its name,' said I; 'prithee be good enough –
    Quick! ere it dart away and disappear.'

And he: 'There doth the ancient spirit rove
    Of criminal Myrrha, who cast amorous eyes
    On her own father with unlawful love,

And in a borrowed frame and false disguise
   Went in to him to do a deed of shame;
   As he that fled but now, to win the prize

"Queen of the Stable", lent his own false frame
   To Buoso de' Donati, and made a will
   In legal form, and forged it in his name.'

So when that rabid pair, on whom I still
   Kept my gaze fixed, had passed, I turned about
   To view those other spirits born for ill;

And saw one there whose shape was like a lute,
   Had but his legs, between the groin and haunch;
   Where the fork comes, been lopt off at the root.

The heavy dropsy, whose indigested bunch
   Of humours bloats the swollen frame within,
   Till the face bears no proportion to the paunch,

Puffed his parched lips apart, with stiffened skin
   Drawn tight, as the hectic gapes, one dry lip curled
   Upward by thirst, the other toward the chin.

'O you,' said he, 'that through this grisly world
   Walk free from punishment – I can't think why –
   Look now and hear; behold the torments hurled

On Master Adam! All that wealth could buy
   Was mine; and now, one drop of water fills
   My craving mind – one drop! O misery!

The little brooks that ripple from the hills
   Of the green Casentin to Arno river,
   Suppling their channels with their cooling rills,

Are in my eyes and in my ears for ever;
   And not for naught – their image dries me more
   Than the disease that wastes my face's favour.

Strict, searching justice balances my score:
   The very land I sinned in has been turned
   To account, to make my sighs more swiftly pour.

Romena's there, the city where I learned
   To falsify the Baptist's coin; up yonder,
   For that offence, I was condemned and burned.

But might I here see Guido or Alexander
   Damned, or their brother, I would not miss that sight
   For all the water in the fount of Branda.

One's here already, if those mad spirits are right
   Who circle all the track; but what's the good
   Of that to me, whose legs are tied so tight?

Were I but still so active that I could
   Drag myself only an inch in a hundred years,
   I'd be on the road by now, be sure I would,

To seek him out from all these sufferers
   Disfigured and maimed, though it's half a mile across
   And eleven miles round at least, from all one hears.

They brought me into this gang of ruin and loss,
    They caused me coin the florins that brought me
      hither,
    Whose gold contained three carats by weight of
      dross.'

Then I to him: 'What shades lie there together
    Rolled in a heap on thy right – that abject pair
    Who smoke as a washed hand smokes in wintry
      weather?'

'When I tumbled into this coop I found them there,'
    Said he, 'and they've never given a turn or kick,
    Nor will to all eternity, I dare swear.

Sinon of Troy is one, the lying Greek;
    One, the false wife who lyingly accused
    Joseph; their burning fever makes them reek.'

Then, vexed belike to hear his name thus used
    Slightingly, one of those shadows seemed to come
    To life and fetched him a walloping blow, fist closed,

On the rigid belly, which thudded back like a drum;
    So Master Adam lammed him over the face
    With an arm as hard as his own, and hit him plumb.

'See now,' said he, 'though I cannot shift my place,
    Because my legs are heavy, yet if need be
    My arm is free, and I keep it ready, in case.'

And he: 'It was not so ready and not so free
    When they haled thee off to the fire; it was free to do
    Thy dirty job of coining – there I agree.'

Then he of the dropsy: 'Now thou speakest true;
    But when at Troy they called on thee to tell
    The truth, thy truthfulness was less in view.'

'If I spoke false, thy coins were false as well;
    I uttered but one lie,' quoth Sinon, 'thou
    Hast uttered more than any fiend in Hell.'

'Perjurer, think of the horse, think of thy vow
    Forsworn,' retorted the blown belly; 'howl
    For grief to think the whole world knows it now.'

'Howl for the thirst that cracks thy tongue, the foul
    Water that bloats thy paunch,' the Greek replied,
    'To a hedge that walls thine eyes and hides thy jowl.'

To whom the coiner: 'Ay, thy mouth gapes wide
    As ever with evil words; if I feel thirst,
    And watery humours stuff me up inside,

Thou burnest, and thy head aches fit to burst;
    Hadst thou Narcissus' mirror there, we'd see
    Thee lap it up and need no prompting first.'

I was all agog and listening eagerly,
    When the master said: 'Yes, feast thine eyes; go on;
    A little more, and I shall quarrel with thee.'

And when I heard him use that angry tone
　　To me, I turned to him so on fire with shame,
　　It comes over me still, though all these years have
　　　flown.

And like a man who dreams a dreadful dream,
　　And dreams he would it were a dream indeed,
　　Longing for that which is, with eager aim

As though 'twere not; so I, speechless to plead
　　For pardon, pleaded all the while with him
　　By my distress, and did not know I did.

'Less shame would wash away a greater crime
　　Than thine has been'; so said my gentle guide;
　　'Think no more of it; but another time,

Imagine I'm still standing at thy side
　　Whenever Fortune, in thy wayfaring,
　　Brings thee where people wrangle thus and chide;

It's vulgar to enjoy that kind of thing.'

[. . .]

Canto XXXII

The Story. *The Tenth Circle is the frozen Lake of Cocytus, which fills the bottom of the Pit, and holds the souls of the Traitors. In the outermost region, Caïna, are the betrayers of their own kindred, plunged to the neck in ice; here Dante sees the Alberti brothers, and speaks with Camicion dei Pazzi. In the next, Antenora, he sees and lays violent hands on Bocca degli Abati, who names various other betrayers of their country; and a little further on he comes upon two other shades, frozen together in the same hole, one of whom is gnawing the head of the other.*

Had I but rhymes rugged and harsh and hoarse,
    Fit for the hideous hole on which the weight
    Of all those rocks grinds downward course by course,

I might press out my matter's juice complete;
    As 'tis, I tremble lest the telling mar
    The tale; for, truly, to describe the great

Fundament of the world is very far
    From being a task for idle wits at play,
    Or infant tongues that pipe *mamma, papa.*

But may those heavenly ladies aid my lay
    That helped Amphion wall high Thebes with stone,
    Lest from the truth my wandering verses stray.

O well for you, dregs of damnation, thrown
    In that last sink which words are weak to tell,
    Had you lived as sheep or goats in the world of the sun!

When we were down in the deep of the darkling well,
    Under the feet of the giant and yet more low,
    And I still gazed up at the towering walls of Hell,

I heard it said: 'Take heed how thou dost go,
    For fear thy feet should trample as they pass
    On the heads of the weary brotherhood of woe.'

I turned and saw, stretched out before my face
    And 'neath my feet, a lake so bound with ice,
    It did not look like water but like glass.

Danube in Austria never could disguise
    His wintry course beneath a shroud so thick
    As this, nor Tanaïs under frozen skies

Afar; if Pietrapan or Tambernic
    Had crashed full weight on it, the very rim
    Would not have given so much as even a creak.

And as with muzzles peeping from the stream
    The frogs sit croaking in the time of year
    When gleaning haunts the peasant-woman's dream,

So, wedged in ice to the point at which appear
   The hues of shame, livid, and with their teeth
   Chattering like storks, the dismal shades stood here.

Their heads were bowed toward the ice beneath,
   Their eyes attest their grief; their mouths proclaim
   The bitter airs that through that dungeon breathe.

My gaze roamed round awhile, and, when it came
   Back to my feet, found two shades so close pressed,
   The hair was mingled on the heads of them.

I said: 'You two, thus cramponed breast to breast,
   Tell me who you are.' They heaved their necks a-strain
   To see me; and as they stood with faces raised,

Their eyes, which were but inly wet till then,
   Gushed at the lids; at once the fierce frost blocked
   The tears between and sealed them shut again.

Never was wood to wood so rigid locked
   By clamps of iron; like butting goats they jarred
   Their heads together, by helpless fury rocked.

Then one who'd lost both ears from off his scarred
   Head with the cold, still keeping his face down,
   Cried out: 'Why dost thou stare at us so hard?

Wouldst learn who those two are? Then be it known,
   They and their father Albert held the valley
   From which the waters of Bisenzio run;

Both of them issued from one mother's belly,
　　Nor shalt thou find, search all Caïna through,
　　Two shades more fit to stand here fixt in jelly;

Not him whose breast and shadow at one blow
　　Were pierced together by the sword of Arthur.
　　Not Focaccìa, nor this other who

So blocks me with his head I see no farther,
　　Called Sassol Mascheroni – if thou be
　　Tuscan, thou know'st him; and I'll tell thee, rather

Than thou shouldst plague me for more speech with
　　　thee,
　　I'm Camicion de' Pazzi, and I wait
　　Till Carlin come to make excuse for me.'

Then I saw thousand faces, and thousands yet,
　　Made doggish with the cold; so that for dread
　　I shudder, and always shall, whenever I set

Eyes on a frozen pool; and as we made
　　Towards the centre where all weights down-weigh,
　　And I was shivering in the eternal shade,

Whether 'twas will, fate, chance, I cannot say,
　　But threading through the heads, I struck my
　　　heel
　　Hard on a face that stood athwart my way.

'Why trample me? What for?' it clamoured shrill;
　'Art come to make the vengeance I endure
　For Montaperti more vindictive still?'

'Master!' I cried, 'wait for me! I adjure
　Thee, wait! Then hurry me on as thou shalt choose;
　But I think I know who it is, and I must make sure.'

The master stopped; and while the shade let loose
　Volleys of oaths: 'Who art thou, cursing so
　And treating people to such foul abuse?'

Said I; and he: 'Nay, who art thou, to go
　Through Antenora, kicking people's faces?
　Thou might'st be living, 'twas so shrewd a blow.'

'Living I am,' said I; 'do thou sing praises
　For that; if thou seek fame, I'll give thee it,
　Writing thy name with other notable cases.'

'All I demand is just the opposite;
　Be off, and pester me no more,' he said;
　'To try such wheedling here shows little wit.'

At that I grasped the scruff behind his head:
　'Thou'lt either tell thy name, or have thy hair
　Stripped from thy scalp,' I panted, 'shred by shred.'

'Pluck it all out,' said he; 'I'll not declare
　My name, nor show my face, though thou insist
　And break my head a thousand times, I swear.'

I'd got his hair twined tightly in my fist
    Already, and wrenched away a tuft or two,
    He yelping, head down, stubborn to resist,

When another called: 'Hey, Bocca, what's to do?
    Don't thy jaws make enough infernal clatter
    But, what the devil! must thou start barking too?'

'There, that's enough,' said I, 'thou filthy traitor;
    Thou need'st not speak; but to thy shame I'll see
    The whole world hears true tidings of this matter.'

'Away, and publish what thou wilt!' said he;
    'But prithee do not fail to advertise
    That chatterbox there, if thou from hence go free.

He wails the Frenchmen's *argent*, treason's price;
    'Him of Duera,' thou shalt say, 'right clear
    I saw, where sinners are preserved in ice.'

And if they should inquire who else was there,
    Close by thee's Beccaria, whose throat was cut
    By Florentines; Gianni de' Soldanier

Is somewhat further on, I fancy, put
    With Ganelon, and Tibbald, who undid
    Faenza's gates when sleeping eyes were shut.'

And when we'd left him, in that icy bed,
    I saw two frozen together in one hole
    So that the one head capped the other head;

And as starved men tear bread, this tore the poll
 Of the one beneath, chewing with ravenous jaw,
 Where brain meets marrow, just beneath the skull.

With no more furious zest did Tydeus gnaw
 The scalp of Menalippus, than he ate
 The brain-pan and the other tissues raw.

'O thou that in such bestial wise dost sate
 Thy rage on him thou munchest, tell me why;
 On this condition,' I said, 'that if thy hate

Seem justified, I undertake that I,
 Knowing who you are, and knowing all his crime,
 Will see thee righted in the world on high,

Unless my tongue wither before the time.'

Canto XXXIII

The Story. *Having heard Count Ugolino's ghastly story of his death by famine, the Poets pass on to Ptolomaea, where Fra Alberigo is cheated by Dante into telling him about himself and Branca d'Oria and others who enjoy the terrible 'privilege' of Ptolomaea.*

Lifting his mouth up from the horrid feast,
    The sinner wiped it on the hair that grew
    Atop the head whose rear he had laid waste;

Then he began: 'Thou bid'st me to renew
    A grief so desperate that the thought alone,
    Before I voice it, cracks my heart in two.

Yet, if indeed my words, like seedlings sown,
    Shall fruit, to shame this traitor whom I tear,
    Then shalt thou see me speak and weep in one.

What man thou art, or what hath brought thee here
    I know not; but I judge thee Florentine,
    If I can trust the witness of my ear.

First learn our names: I was Count Ugolino,
    And he, Archbishop Roger; hearken well
    Wherefore I use him thus, this neighbour of mine.

That once I trusted him, and that I fell
  Into the snare that he contrived somehow,
  And so was seized and slain, I need not tell.

What thou canst not have learned, I'll tell thee now:
  How bitter cruel my death was; hear, and then,
  If he has done me injury, judge thou.

A narrow loophole in the dreadful den
  Called "Famine" after me, and which, meseems,
  Shall be a dungeon yet for many men,

Had filtered through to me the pallid gleams
  Of many changing moons, before one night
  Unveiled the future to my haunted dreams.

I saw this man, a lord and master of might,
  Chasing the wolf and wolf-cubs on the hill
  Which shuts out Lucca from the Pisans' sight.

His hounds were savage, swift and keen of skill,
  And many a Sismund, Gualand and Lanfranc,
  Like huntsmen, rode before him to the kill.

I saw how father and sons wearied and sank
  After a short quick run; I saw the dread
  Sharp teeth that tore at bleeding throat and flank.

And waking early ere the dawn was red
  I heard my sons, who were with me, in their sleep
  Weeping aloud and crying out for bread.

Think what my heart misgave; and if thou keep
    From tears, thou art right cruel; if thou for this
    Weep not, at what then art thou wont to weep?

By now they'd waked; the hour at which our mess
    Was daily brought drew near; ill dreams had stirred
    Our hearts and filled us with unquietness.

Then at the foot of that grim tower I heard
    Men nailing up the gate, far down below;
    I gazed in my sons' eyes without a word;

I wept not; I seemed turned to stone all through;
    They wept; I heard my little Anselm say:
    "Father, what's come to thee? Why look'st thou so?"

I shed no tear, nor answered, all that day
    Nor the next night, until another sun
    Rose on the world. And when the first faint ray

Stole through into that dismal cell of stone,
    And eyeing those four faces I could see
    In every one the image of my own,

I gnawed at both my hands for misery;
    And they, who thought it was for hunger plain
    And simple, rose at once and said to me:

"O Father, it will give us much less pain
    If thou wilt feed on us; thy gift at birth
    Was this sad flesh, strip thou it off again."

To spare them grief I calmed myself. Hard earth,
   Hadst thou no pity? couldst thou not gape wide?
   That day and next we all sat mute. The fourth,

Crept slowly in on us. Then Gaddo cried,
   And dropped down at my feet: "My father, why
   Dost thou not help me?" So he said, and died.

As thou dost see me here, I saw him die,
   And one by one the other three died too,
   From the fifth day to the sixth. Already I

Was blind; I took to fumbling them over; two
   Long days I groped there, calling on the dead;
   Then famine did what sorrow could not do.'

He ceased, and rolled his eyes asquint, and sped
   To plant his teeth, which, like a dog's, were strong
   Upon the bone, back in the wretched head.

O Pisa! scandal of all folk whose tongue
   In our fair country speaks the sound of *si*,
   Since thy dull neighbours will not smite such wrong

With vengeance, move Gorgona from the sea,
   Caprara move, and dam up Arno's mouth,
   Till every living soul is drowned in thee!

For though Count Ugolino in very truth
   Betrayed thee of thy castles, it was crime
   To torture those poor children; tender youth,

O cruel city, Thebes of modern time,
   Made Hugh and Il Brigata innocent
   And the other two whose names are in my rhyme.

We passed; and found, as further on we went,
   A people fettered in the frost's rough grip,
   Flat on their backs, instead of forward bent.

There the mere weeping will not let them weep,
   For grief, which finds no outlet at the eyes,
   Turns inward to make anguish drive more deep;

For their first tears freeze to a lump of ice
   Which like a crystal mask fills all the space
   Beneath the brows and plugs the orifice.

And now, although, as from a calloused place,
   By reason of the cold that pinched me so,
   All feeling had departed from my face,

I felt as 'twere a wind begin to blow.
   Wherefore I said: 'Master, what makes it move?
   Is not all heat extinguished here below?'

'Thine eyes,' said he, 'shall answer soon enough;
   We're coming to the place from which the blast
   Pours down, and thou shalt see the cause thereof.'

And one of the wretched whom the frost holds fast
   Cried out: 'O souls so wicked that of all
   The posts of Hell you hold the very last,

Rend from my face this rigid corporal,
   That I may vent my stuffed heart at my eyes
   Once, though the tears refreeze before they fall.'

Then I: 'Tell me thy name: that is my price
   For help; and if I do not set thee free,
   May I be sent to the bottom of the ice.'

And he: 'I am Friar Alberigo, he
   Of the fruits of the ill garden; in this bed
   Dates for my figs are given back to me.'

'How now,' said I, 'art thou already dead?'
   And in reply: 'Nay, how my body fares
   In the upper world I do not know,' he said.

'Such privilege this Ptolomaea bears
   That oft the soul falls down here ere the day
   When Atropos compels it with her shears.

And, if it will persuade thee take away
   These glazing tears by which my face is screened,
   Know, when a soul has chosen to betray,

As I did, straight it's ousted by a fiend,
   Who takes and rules the body till the full
   Term of its years has circled to an end.

The soul drops down into this cistern-pool;
   Belike the shade wintering behind me here
   Still has a body on earth – it's probable

Thou'lt know, if thou art new come down from there;
    He is Ser Branca d'Oria; in this pit's
    Cold storage he has lain this many a year.'

'I think,' said I, 'that these are pure deceits,
    For Branca d'Oria has by no means died;
    He wears his clothes and sleeps and drinks and eats.'

'Up in that moat where the Hellrakers bide,'
    He answered, 'Michael Zanche'd not yet come
    To boil and bubble in the tarry tide

When this man left a devil in his room,
    In his flesh and that kinsman's flesh, whom he
    Joined with himself in treachery, and in doom.

And now, do thou stretch forth thy hand to me,
    Undo my eyes.' And I undid them not,
    And churlishness to him was courtesy.

O Genoa, where hearts corrupt and rot,
    Lost to all decency! will no man hound
    Thy whole tribe from the earth and purge this blot?

For with Romagna's vilest spirit I found
    One of such rank deeds, such a Genoan,
    His soul bathes in Cocytus, while on ground

His body walks and seems a living man.

Canto XXXIV

The Story. *After passing over the region of Judecca, where the Traitors to their Lords are wholly immersed in the ice, the Poets see Dis (Satan) devouring the shades of Judas, Brutus, and Cassius. They clamber along his body until, passing through the centre of the Earth, they emerge into a rocky cavern. From here they follow the stream of Lethe upwards until it brings them out on the island of Mount Purgatory in the Antipodes.*

'*Vexilla regis prodeunt inferni*
    Encountering us; canst thou distinguish him,
    Look forward,' said the master, 'as we journey.'

As, when a thick mist breathes, or when the rim
    Of night creeps up across our hemisphere,
    A turning windmill looms in the distance dim,

I thought I saw a shadowy mass appear;
    Then shrank behind my leader from the blast,
    Because there was no other cabin here.

I stood (with fear I write it) where at last
    The shades, quite covered by the frozen sheet,
    Gleamed through the ice like straws in crystal
        glassed;

Some lie at length and others stand in it,
   This one upon his head, and that upright,
   Another like a bow bent face to feet.

And when we had come so far that it seemed right
   To my dear master, he should let me see
   That creature fairest once of the sons of light,

He moved him from before me and halted me,
   And said: 'Behold now Dis! behold the place
   Where thou must steel thy soul with constancy.'

How cold I grew, how faint with fearfulness,
   Ask me not, Reader; I shall not waste breath
   Telling what words are powerless to express;

This was not life, and yet it was not death;
   If thou hast wit to think how I might fare
   Bereft of both, let fancy aid thy faith.

The Emperor of the sorrowful realm was there,
   Out of the girding ice he stood breast-high,
   And to his arm alone the giants were

Less comparable than to a giant I;
   Judge then how huge the stature of the whole
   That to so huge a part bears symmetry.

If he was once as fair as now he's foul,
   And dared outface his Maker in rebellion,
   Well may he be the fount of all our dole.

And marvel 'twas, out-marvelling a million,
　　When I beheld three faces in his head;
　　The one in front was scarlet like vermilion;

And two, mid-centred on the shoulders, made
　　Union with this, and each with either fellow
　　Knit at the crest, in triune junction wed.

The right was of a hue 'twixt white and yellow;
　　The left was coloured like the men who dwell
　　Where Nile runs down from source to sandy shallow.

From under each sprang two great wings that well
　　Befitted such a monstrous bird as that;
　　I ne'er saw ship with such a spread of sail.

Plumeless and like the pinions of a bat
　　Their fashion was; and as they flapped and whipped
　　Three winds went rushing over the icy flat

And froze up all Cocytus; and he wept
　　From his six eyes, and down his triple chin
　　Runnels of tears and bloody slaver dripped.

Each mouth devoured a sinner clenched within,
　　Frayed by the fangs like flax beneath a brake;
　　Three at a time he tortured them for sin.

But all the bites the one in front might take
　　Were nothing to the claws that flayed his hide
　　And sometimes stripped his back to the last flake.

'That wretch up there whom keenest pangs divide
   Is Judas called Iscariot,' said my lord,
   'His head within, his jerking legs outside;

As for the pair whose heads hang hitherward;
   From the black mouth the limbs of Brutus sprawl –
   See how he writhes and utters never a word;

And strong-thewed Cassius is his fellow-thrall.
   But come; for night is rising on the world
   Once more; we must depart; we have seen all.'

Then, as he bade, about his neck I curled
   My arms and clasped him. And he spied the time
   And place; and when the wings were wide unfurled

Set him upon the shaggy flanks to climb,
   And thus from shag to shag descended down
   'Twixt matted hair and crusts of frozen rime.

And when we had come to where the huge thigh-bone
   Rides in its socket at the haunch's swell,
   My guide, with labour and great exertion,

Turned head to where his feet had been, and fell
   To hoisting himself up upon the hair,
   So that I thought us mounting back to Hell.

'Hold fast to me, for by so steep a stair,'
   My master said, panting like one forspent,
   'Needs must we quit this realm of all despair.'

At length, emerging through a rocky vent,
   He perched me sitting on the rim of the cup
   And crawled out after, heedful how he went.

I raised my eyes, thinking to see the top
   Of Lucifer, as I had left him last;
   But only saw his great legs sticking up.

And if I stood dumbfounded and aghast,
   Let those thick-witted gentry judge and say,
   Who do not see what point it was I'd passed.

'Up on thy legs!' the master said; 'the way
   Is long, the road rough going for the feet,
   And at mid-terce already stands the day.'

The place we stood in was by no means fit
   For a king's palace, but a natural prison,
   With a vile floor, and very badly lit.

'One moment, sir,' said I, when I had risen;
   'Before I pluck myself from the Abyss,
   Lighten my darkness with a word in season.

Kindly explain; what's happened to the ice?
   What's turned him upside-down? or in an hour
   Thus whirled the sun from dusk to dawning skies?'

'Thou think'st,' he said, 'thou standest as before
   You side the centre, where I grasped the hair
   Of the ill Worm that pierces the world's core.

So long as I descended, thou wast there;
   But when I turned, then was the point passed by
   Toward which all weight bears down from everywhere.

The other hemisphere doth o'er thee lie –
   Antipodal to that which land roofs in,
   And under whose meridian came to die

The Man born sinless and who did no sin;
   Thou hast thy feet upon a little sphere
   Of whose far side Judecca forms the skin.

When it is evening there, it's morning here;
   And he whose pelt our ladder was, stands still
   Fixt in the self-same place, and does not stir.

This side the world from out high Heaven he fell;
   The land which here stood forth fled back dismayed,
   Pulling the sea upon her like a veil,

And sought our hemisphere; with equal dread,
   Belike, that peak of earth which still is found
   This side, rushed up, and so this void was made.'

There is a place low down there underground,
   As far from Belzebub as his tomb's deep,
   Not known to sight, but only by the sound

Of a small stream which trickles down the steep,
   Hollowing its channel, where with gentle fall
   And devious course its wandering waters creep.

By that hid way my guide and I withal,
    Back to the lit world from the darkened dens
    Toiled upward, caring for no rest at all,

He first, I following; till my straining sense
    Glimpsed the bright burden of the heavenly cars
    Through a round hole; by this we climbed, and
        thence

Came forth, to look once more upon the stars.